A Soldier's Friend

Praise for Megan Rix:

'If you love Michael Morpurgo, you'll enjoy this' *Sunday Express*

'A moving tale told with warmth, kindliness and lashings of good sense that lovers of Dick King-Smith will especially appreciate' *The Times*

'Every now and then a writer comes along with a unique way of storytelling . . . Meet Megan Rix . . . her novels are deeply moving and will strike a chord with animal lovers' LoveReading.com

Praise from Megan's young readers:

'I never liked reading until one day I was in Waterstones and I picked up some books. One was . . . called *The Bomber Dog*. I loved it so much I couldn't put it down' Luke, 8

'I found this book amazing' Nayah, 11

'EPIC BOOK!!!' Jessica, 13

'One of my favourite books' Chloe, 12

'I swear this is the best story I have ever read in my entire life' Rashmi, 10

MEGAN RIX lives with her husband by a river in England. When she's not writing she can be found walking her two golden retrievers, Traffy and Bella, who are often in the river.

Books by Megan Rix

THE BOMBER DOG

THE GREAT ESCAPE

A SOLDIER'S FRIEND

THE VICTORY DOGS

Don't miss Megan's exciting new story, publishing in autumn 2014.

www.meganrix.com

The little creature was running for all he was worth, hopping, jumping, plunging, all with the most obvious concentration of purpose . . .

– British War Dogs, Their Training and Psychology, Lt.-Col E. H. Richardson

EUROPE 1914

KEY

GERMANY AND ITS ALLIES

BRITAIN AND ITS ALLIES

NEUTRAL

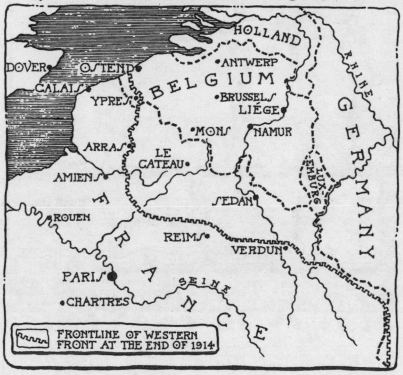

THE WESTERN FRONT

HOLLAND

DOVER
CALAIS
OSTEND
YPRES
ARRAS
AMIENS
ROUEN
PARIS
CHARTRES

BELGIUM

ANTWERP
BRUSSELS
LIÉGE
MONS
LE CATEAU
NAMUR
SEDAN
REIMS
VERDUN

FRANCE

SEINE

GERMANY

RHINE
LUXEMBURG

FRONTLINE OF WESTERN
FRONT AT THE END OF 1914

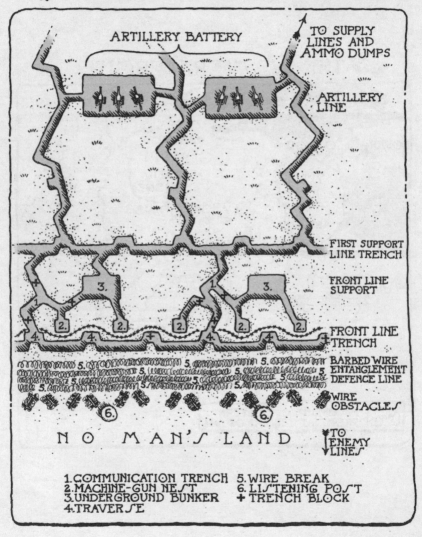

TRENCH WARFARE SYSTEM

ARTILLERY BATTERY

TO SUPPLY LINES AND AMMO DUMPS

ARTILLERY LINE

FIRST SUPPORT LINE TRENCH

FRONT LINE SUPPORT

3.

1.

FRONT LINE TRENCH

BARBED WIRE ENTANGLEMENT DEFENCE LINE

WIRE OBSTACLES

6.

NO MAN'S LAND

TO ENEMY LINES

1. COMMUNICATION TRENCH
2. MACHINE-GUN NEST
3. UNDERGROUND BUNKER
4. TRAVERSE

5. WIRE BREAK
6. LISTENING POST
+ TRENCH BLOCK

CROSS-SECTION OF BRITISH TRENCH 1914

BARBED WIRE

PARAPET

ELBOW REST

AMMUNITION SHELF

FIRESTEP

DUCKBOARDS

SUMP

0.5m

SANDBAGS

DUGOUT

2.0 metres

Chapter 1

The little shaggy-coated cairn terrier puppy trotted down the cobblestoned street in the late afternoon sunshine. Every now and again he looked up at his owner through the grey fur that half flopped over one of his eyes and his little tail wagged happily. But the man didn't reach down and pat him like the little dog wanted him to. He didn't even look at the pup.

'This'll do as well as any,' the man muttered gruffly as they came to a stop outside a large grey building that loomed above them with a sign in front of it saying BATTERSEA MUNITIONS FACTORY.

The small puppy looked up expectantly with his head cocked to one side. His tail still wagged while his lead was tied to a post. Perhaps this was a new game? He tried to lick his owner's hand, but was brushed away.

'None of that now,' the man muttered briskly.

The puppy sat down. He watched as the man stood up and turned away. Then the little dog jumped up and tried to follow his owner as he headed off down the street, but a second later the little pup was jerked back by his lead. He pulled again, as hard as he could, twisting this way and that, but he couldn't get loose. He barked and then he barked again, now desperate, but his owner didn't come back.

Further along the street, just around the corner, nineteen-year-old Oliver Peters paused before kicking the football into the improvised goal marked out with his cap and his friend's jacket. There it was again, that strange cry. It sounded like some kind of animal. *A dog*, he thought. *A dog in distress*.

Oliver frowned; he hated any animal to be frightened or in pain. He tried to work out which direction the sound had come from, but the high yap didn't come again and he assumed the dog's owner must have returned.

Fourteen-year-old Ivor interrupted the hush that had descended on the fifteen or so men and boys who were playing the game, as they waited for Oliver to shoot.

'Get on with it,' he shouted from the front garden wall that he was sitting on.

'The enemy would have got him by now,' Ivor's friend Thumbs, also on the wall, agreed.

'Yeah,' Ivor snickered. 'You're going to lose the war for us, you are, Oliver.'

Oliver didn't even hear Ivor as he worked

out the best angle for his shot. The two things he loved most were animals and football.

'Shut up, you two,' Patrick told Ivor and Thumbs, coming over to them.

Patrick was the same age as Oliver, and his best friend. They were apprentices at the same factory, lived in the same digs and had joined up to fight in the war at Battersea Recruiting Depot on the same day, as had most of the others who were playing. This was their last game before they left for the Western Front in the morning. All over the country, men had been encouraged to join up together and form what everyone called 'PALs battalions'.

The Secretary of State for War, Lord Kitchener, had promised they could serve alongside their friends, neighbours and work colleagues, rather than being allocated to regular army regiments. Hundreds of PALs battalions had formed to swell the ranks and now those that were old enough in the Battersea Beasts football team would join them.

'We're only ribbing him,' Ivor said to Patrick. 'Can't he take a joke?'

'Just because you're too young to sign up doesn't mean you need to make fun of the rest of us who are going,' Patrick told him.

'It's OK, Patrick, they just want to be part of England's victory, like we do!' said Oliver as he expertly kicked the ball straight into the goal that eleven-year-old Arthur was guarding.

'Nooooo!' Arthur shouted as he watched the ball bounce cleanly between the cap and jacket.

From her open bedroom window upstairs, Arthur's twelve-year-old sister Lizzie saw the goal being scored.

'Nice goal, Oliver,' she said, although of course he couldn't hear her. Lizzie really liked Oliver. He always included her younger brother

Arthur in the football games, and treated him like one of the older boys from the neighbourhood, even though he was only eleven. Ever since their dad had died a few years earlier, Lizzie knew how much Arthur depended on Oliver's friendship. They all did, even Mum, so much so that Lizzie thought of him as part of their family now.

She went back to putting her long, just washed and still damp red hair in curling rags. The six-inch-long strips of white sheeting were being awkward as she wound strands of her hair round them. She'd much rather have been outside playing football with her brother.

A large grey tabby cat jumped up on to the window sill next to Lizzie and, with a quick miaow, ducked out of the window.

'Have fun, Mouser,' Lizzie said as she watched her cat nimbly make her way to the ground via eave and lilac bush. A moment later Mouser was heading off down the street and evading the hands of the footballers that tried to stroke her.

'Here, puss . . .'

'She only lets people stroke her when she wants to be stroked,' Arthur told them.

'Come on, Thumbs,' Ivor said as he hopped off the garden wall. He knew they couldn't take Patrick on, much as they liked making snarky comments. Often they joined in with the other lads playing football on the street, but today the game had already begun by the time Ivor and Thumbs arrived.

Ivor kicked a pebble to Thumbs and Thumbs kicked it back as they headed towards the station along the cobblestoned street.

'One shilling a day they're going to be getting paid, at least,' Ivor said. 'One whole shilling for joining the army.'

'It isn't fair that we're not allowed to go to war too,' muttered Thumbs, who was even younger than Ivor.

As the two boys passed by the entrance to the large munitions factory, they didn't hear the puppy's faint whimper as he lay down on the pavement and rested his head on his paws.

An hour passed, two hours, three, and the puppy remained tethered to the post by the factory gate. When the whistle blew for the end of the shift, he was still there.

Exhausted women hurried past the little dog without knowing how long he'd been tied up. A few of them commented on how sweet he was as they made their weary way home.

'Look at his beautiful brown eyes . . .'

'Poor little fella, do you think he's all alone?'

'At any other time I'd stop to find out, but there's a war on . . . we can't afford to worry about stray animals.'

Ever since war had been declared, there'd been a frenzy of activity as men enlisted and were trained to fight and women took over the jobs they'd left behind. There were women working in the factories and delivering groceries and coal. Some of them even worked down the mines. YOUR COUNTRY NEEDS YOU posters were everywhere and more than half the male teachers at Arthur and Lizzie's school had already left for the front so the female teachers now taught their classes as well as their own.

The street grew quiet as the factory emptied and the puppy was quite alone again. As the sky grew darker, he tugged at his lead once more. It was frayed now, but he still couldn't break free. He chewed on it with his sharp puppy teeth.

The warmth of the day passed and he shivered in the cold as a storm threatened.

Mouser was a cat that wasn't afraid of anything she encountered on her nightly prowls, and certainly not a puppy. She stalked over to him to investigate as he jumped up, wagged his tail excitedly and yapped, jumping round the large grey tabby as far as his chewed lead would let him.

Suddenly the little pup went deathly still at the sound of a distant rumble of thunder. He began to pant nervously as Mouser watched him with her green eyes, her tail twitching slowly. Storms and thunder held no fear for her. The puppy yelped and cowered away as the thunder came again. It was closer this time and followed by a flash of white lightning. The little dog twisted and turned. He tugged with all his might against his lead and finally it broke and he toppled over with the shock of being so suddenly released. A moment later he'd scrambled to his feet as the thunder thudded through the sky once again. And then he was off, running, not thinking, not knowing where he was going, just needing to get away from the storm.

Mouser watched the puppy, hesitated for a second and then followed as he ran along the pavement and out on to the road in a panic.

He didn't see the rag-and-bone man's cart or the horse drawing it until it was too late.

'Whoa there!' the rag-and-bone man shouted as the horse shied away rather than step on the small dog.

The puppy rolled on to his back, showing his tummy in a sign of submission as he stared up at the huge beast, too petrified to move.

'Go on – get out of it!' the man shouted. It had been a very long day and he'd no intention of getting down from the cart for anyone or anything until they were back at the yard.

Mouser ran into the road and nudged the puppy out of the way as the horse clopped on. Heavy spots of rain began to fall and the puppy followed Mouser as she led him to shelter in a blackberry bush in an alleyway nearby. His little body trembled with fear as they huddled close together until the storm was over. Mouser licked the puppy's head with her raspy tongue to comfort him and finally the exhausted little dog fell asleep as she watched over him.

Just before dawn the puppy stirred and, still half asleep, began chewing on the nearest thing to him, which happened to be Mouser's ear.

Mouser gave a warning miaow and the puppy's brown eyes opened. He looked at his new friend and his little wail wagged. Now he was fully awake and ready to play. He jumped up and put his paw out to Mouser. Mouser's tail twitched and soon the two of them were running up and down the alleyway in a game of chase, as the puppy yipped with delight.

Five minutes later they returned to the blackberry bush and the puppy flopped down while Mouser looked over at the upstairs window of the Jensons' house opposite. The puppy stood up to follow her as she made her way to the back garden fence. He didn't want to be left behind, but Mouser turned and nuzzled her face to his, ushering him back to the blackberry bush.

He watched Mouser jump easily over the back garden fence. Then he made a soft whimpering sound, curled up and went back to sleep.

Mrs Jenson was already up and in the kitchen at the back of the house. It was just after 5 a.m. and she needed to leave for work at the factory at 5.30. Thousands of women had flocked to the munitions factories to help make the ammunition that was needed for the war. Some of the other women who worked there had begun to wear overalls and trousers with tunics over them, but Mrs Jenson preferred her overall dress and cap. Everyone had to wear protective clothing because of the danger from the chemicals they were working with, and the cap was worn so strands of their hair didn't get caught in the machinery.

'Morning, Mouser,' Mrs Jenson said as the cat came in through the window.

Mouser let Mrs Jenson stroke her a few times before she slipped away and headed upstairs to her favourite bed for a nap.

Chapter 2

The puppy was well hidden in the midst of the overgrown blackberry bush that spread the length of the narrow alleyway at the back of the row of houses. People passed close by him on their way to work without realizing he was even there. When he woke for the second time, he watched them from his new den with his sharp button-brown eyes. He felt safe hidden among the leaves, but he was hungry, very hungry. He looked over at the back fence where his new friend had gone and whined.

Upstairs in Lizzie's bedroom, on Lizzie's bed, lay Mouser. As usual, she'd made herself very comfortable, taking far more than her fair share of the pillow. Lizzie's hair was covered in little strips of white rag tied in knots. Mouser watched the rags going up and down as Lizzie breathed deeply in and out, fast asleep. She batted at a thread hanging from one of the rags with her paw. Lizzie slept on. Mouser batted at another of the shivering rags and caught Lizzie's nose.

'Ouch!' Lizzie cried, and she opened her eyes. 'What did you do that for?'

Mouser didn't have an answer, but simply jumped off the bed and stalked out of the door.

Lizzie sighed and pulled back the bedclothes. She heard the clatter of cups down in the kitchen and went to join her mother. Mouser was already there.

'Do you know what Mouser just did? She batted me on the nose, on purpose.'

Mrs Jenson smiled at her outraged daughter. 'I'm sure it wasn't on purpose,' she said. 'Mouser's just a cat after all.'

But Lizzie wasn't so sure about that. The nose bat had felt very purposeful to her.

Her mother handed Lizzie a cup of tea and then she poured another one from the large brown china pot.

'I'm taking this up to your brother. Oliver's about to pop in to say goodbye to him,' she said as she picked the cups up. 'That poor boy, going off to war . . .'

'Arthur's probably still asleep,' Lizzie said. She added a little more sugar to her tea as soon as her mother left the room. She'd be asleep too if it wasn't for Mouser.

Mouser came over and curled herself round Lizzie's legs and purred. Lizzie reached down to stroke her. 'Yes, of course I forgive you,' she said as if the cat had asked her. 'But it's not very nice being batted awake by a paw, let me tell you.'

She lifted Mouser on to her lap. Sometimes Mouser let herself be stroked and sometimes she didn't. It all depended on how she was feeling at the time. But they were all going to want to stroke the cat today, especially her brother Arthur, because Oliver was leaving to go to war. No one really wanted him to. Oliver had worked as their father's apprentice before their father passed away and had been a good friend to the family ever since. He was like part of their family now and they were all going to miss him badly.

Lizzie sighed as Mouser jumped off her lap and headed up the stairs to her brother's room.

'Thanks, Mum,' Arthur said as he took his tea. He moved the cup swiftly out of the way so Mouser wouldn't bump into it as she jumped up on to his bed, light as a feather for such a big cat.

Mouser kneaded the covers with her paws, making herself a comfortable spot, and lay down just as there was a knock at the front door.

'That'll be Oliver,' said Arthur, and he jumped up to rush downstairs, followed by Mouser.

'Morning all,' said Oliver cheerily. He put his kitbag and the football he was holding by the front door. 'Oh, and hello, Mouser,' he said as Mouser wrapped herself round one of his legs. He reached down and stroked her.

'It's like she knows this is your last day,' Arthur said, although he knew she couldn't really.

'I saw a poster yesterday outside the station asking for cats to be donated to the war effort,' Mrs Jenson said.

'I don't think Mouser would like to go to

war,' said Oliver. 'Would you, Mouser?' He smoothed his fingers along the fur of her back.

Arthur frowned. 'But why would they want cats to go to war?'

'Apparently they make good rat-catchers in the trenches, or so they say,' Mrs Jenson told him.

Arthur couldn't really imagine Mouser helping the Allies to win the war against Germany. She wasn't the type of cat to obey orders. And what could a cat possibly do anyway? Not a lot, in his opinion. It wasn't like the horses that were going off to war. He could see how they would be useful leading the battle charge. He could see himself sitting on one, with his sword raised, as they raced together to take down the enemy.

Not that he'd ever been on a horse, but he was sure they couldn't be that hard to ride. He smiled to himself as he took a swig of his tea.

Arthur spent a lot of time imagining life

as a soldier. Most of the time he saw himself as an infantryman like Oliver had been trained to be. But sometimes he pictured himself riding a horse or being a spy or driving one of the cars. Not that he'd ever been in a car, and there weren't that many about, but he was sure he'd be able to drive one if he did get the chance. He even tried to imagine himself as a pilot of one of the planes he'd seen a picture of in the newspaper, although that wasn't quite as easy to do.

As soon as Oliver and his friends had arrived home from the army training camp last week, Arthur had made Oliver tell him absolutely everything about it.

'What did you have to eat?'

'Bully beef and plum duff.'

'How many other soldiers were there?'

'Too many to count.'

'What name was your battalion given?'

'We were allowed to choose our own.

Battersea Chums didn't sound quite right and nor did Battersea Brigade, and Battersea Boys was too childish . . .'

'So?'

'We chose Battersea Beasts.'

Arthur's eyes had opened wide.

'Just like our football team!'

The name sounded perfect. He hoped the war wasn't already over by the time he was old enough to join the Battersea Beasts. But everyone said it'd be done by Christmas and that was only three months away, so it didn't seem very likely.

'What did you have to do at camp all day?'

When Oliver told him how they had to run at a potato sack filled with sand and poke at it with the blade stuck to the end of their rifle, called a bayonet, Arthur had run straight to the greengrocer's and begged him for a spare potato sack so he could have one just the same. He'd filled it with soil as he didn't have any sand. He didn't have a rifle or a bayonet either, so he ran at it with the broom instead. There wasn't much space to do that in their tiny back garden, but he managed, just about.

When he told his friends about it, everyone wanted to have a go and there was even less space in the garden when they were there too.

'We're going to miss you,' Lizzie said to Oliver as she came into the kitchen, her voice catching in her throat; saying out loud the words she'd been thinking made her realize just how much. She plonked herself down on a chair and picked up Mouser.

Mouser let herself be stroked, while gazing wistfully at the window.

'What are you looking at?' Lizzie asked the cat as she followed her gaze.

'Almost time for me to be heading off to work,' Mrs Jenson said sadly. 'I wish I could stay to see you off, Oliver, I really do.'

Oliver didn't have any family of his own and Mrs Jenson thought of him almost as an extra son. But the munitionettes' work was too vital and too urgent for her to be given time off for any reason.

'I don't want anyone seeing me off,' Oliver said firmly. 'I'll have Patrick and the others with me so it's not like I'm heading out to the Western Front alone or with strangers.'

'What is the Western Front exactly?' Lizzie asked Oliver. It was talked about all the time, but not marked on the map at school.

'It's the thin strip of land between Germany, France and Belgium that we're trying to hold, to stop the Germans from making their way through Belgium and into France . . . But you two don't need to worry about that. Now there's one thing I'd like to do before I leave . . .'

'What's that?' Arthur asked him.

'Well, I reckon there won't be much time for football at the front – wouldn't be surprised if there's none at all. So, one last very quick game – it should be light enough to see the ball – before I go?'

He looked at Arthur and Lizzie.

'Course,' Lizzie said.

'Good idea,' said Arthur.

'Take care and come home soon,' Mrs Jenson said as she kissed Oliver on the cheek.

'I will. Don't worry about me.'

Mrs Jenson managed a watery smile as she pulled on her cap and headed off to work.

While Oliver and Arthur quickly finished their tea, Lizzie went back to her room to take the curling rags out of her hair. The curls worked best if she used the rags on wet hair and let it dry overnight.

Mouser miaowed at the window, asking to be let out.

'In a minute,' Lizzie told her as she unravelled more rags. Mouser miaowed again. 'One minute,' Lizzie said. 'What's the rush?'

Downstairs Oliver and Arthur heard a faint, high-pitched yelp.

'Did you hear that?' said Arthur.

'Has someone got a new dog around here?' Oliver asked. 'I thought I heard something similar yesterday when we were playing football. I think it sounds like a dog's bark.'

Oliver knew most of the neighbourhood dogs and recognized their different barks. But this didn't sound the same as the Labrador from two doors along or the poodle that lived above the shop close to the factory. It also sounded very near and much more desperate.

He headed over to the kitchen door.

'Come on,' he said to Arthur.

They hurried out into the garden and over to the back gate that led to the alley behind the house.

'Look! Arthur said. 'I think it's a puppy.'

Oliver was just in time to catch a glimpse of

a grey shaggy coat before it disappeared back underneath the blackberry bush that ran along the alley.

'It's gone.'

Mouser jumped on to the back fence and then down into the alleyway and followed the puppy under the bush.

Oliver grinned. 'Looks like Mouser's made a new friend,' he said.

'It didn't look much bigger than her,' said Arthur. 'Maybe that's why she likes it. Maybe she thinks it's another cat.'

Oliver laughed. 'Whatever she thinks, I bet Mouser's the one who's in charge.'

Both of them knew Mouser was a cat who liked to get her own way; she usually managed it too.

'What type of dog was it?' asked Arthur.

'I couldn't tell, I'm afraid. I only caught a glimpse of its coat.'

'Ready?' Lizzie asked from the garden gate. They never played football in the back garden: it wasn't big enough. So they all headed back into the house, picked up Oliver's football and went out on to the street for one last game under the pink-streaked sky.

Chapter 3

'Flip a coin for who's in goal?' Oliver said. But Arthur knew Oliver liked scoring goals more than saving them.

'I'll be in goal,' he told him.

Lizzie and Oliver played against each other. Oliver had the ball first and dribbled it down the street, but then Lizzie tackled and got it away from him. She dribbled the ball towards Arthur, only to have Oliver take it off her, and then Lizzie got it again. She hesitated as she looked at Arthur in goal, waiting for her to strike. Oliver was leaving. He should be the one scoring.

'Go on, Lizzie,' Oliver said.

And Lizzie shot the ball straight into the goal space with her left foot.

'You're a natural, Lizzie,' Oliver told her, giving her shoulder a squeeze.

Lizzie blushed at the compliment. She loved football, but not many of the other girls played, so she didn't often get the chance.

Arthur kicked the ball back towards Oliver and Oliver dribbled it past Lizzie and kicked it straight into the goal. Then he scored two more goals in quick succession as Arthur groaned. He'd not stood a chance of stopping any of the goals so far. He kicked the ball back out again, but this time Oliver picked it up and kept hold of it.

'Hey, Arthur,' he said and threw his precious leather football to him. 'You and Lizzie should look after this while I'm away. But don't just let it sit on the shelf – it needs to be played with.'

Arthur grinned. 'Don't worry, it will be.'

He was a little surprised Oliver wasn't taking his football with him and hadn't somehow managed to squeeze it in his bag.

'And think about me when you do play,' Oliver added softly. 'I'll be back before Christmas for a rematch and I'll know if you two haven't been practising.'

Then he went back inside to pick up his kitbag.

'Right, it's time I got going.'

Lizzie ran to him and hugged him tightly as he came out of the front door.

'No tears,' Oliver told her.

'No tears,' she said. 'I promise.'

The pink streaks in the sky had faded, leaving only a radiant turquoise-blue morning.

Oliver pumped Arthur's hand up and down in a very grown-up handshake, and then he strode off down the street, whistling, as Lizzie and Arthur waved.

He was meeting the other Battersea Beasts

at the station and he didn't want to be late. They'd been looking forward to this for weeks.

When Lizzie and Arthur couldn't see Oliver any more, they went home to have breakfast and get ready for school.

Neither of them spoke about how much they were going to miss him. It was too painful and raw.

Usually Mouser would be demanding her breakfast by now, but today she wasn't there.

Arthur told Lizzie about Mouser's new friend.

'Looked like a puppy or a very small dog.'

''Spect she'll be back by the time we get home from school,' Lizzie said. It wasn't like Mouser to miss a mealtime.

Ivor and Thumbs were outside the station looking at the cat poster Mrs Jenson had mentioned.

'Say hello to Fritz the German from me,' Ivor said when he saw Oliver.

'Yeah, from me too,' said Thumbs.

'Might be able to say it yourself one day,' Patrick told them, coming over to join Oliver. 'If the army's ever desperate enough to take you two.'

He laughed and gave them a quick wave before heading into the station with Oliver to catch their train.

'Now just you listen . . .' Thumbs said, his chin sticking out and his fists clenched, starting to follow Oliver and Patrick.

But Ivor pulled him away. He'd got a good idea. A way for them to make some much needed cash. He dragged Thumbs down the street to tell him about it.

'If the army's happy enough to pay for all them horses they've been using in the war, why shouldn't they be happy to pay for cats too, especially if we happened to have five or six fine-looking rat-catching beasts all at once?'

Thumbs thought this was an excellent idea

and the two of them set to work finding suitable-looking cats straight away. It wasn't as easy as he'd thought it would be.

'Shame we couldn't get a few from Battersea Dogs Home – bet they've got more than enough cats to spare,' Ivor said, after they'd been cat hunting for a few hours.

'Probably already donated them. Dogs too – I heard they already donated dogs.' Thumbs frowned. 'Why don't they call it Battersea Dogs *and Cats* home when everyone knows they've got cats there as well?'

Ivor shrugged. It didn't make sense to him either.

The wooded areas of Battersea Park were perfect for hunting in and Mouser visited them most days. Not that she needed to hunt for food as she was given more than enough at home and was never hungry. But still she came. Today the puppy trotted along beside her, his little tail wagging excitedly, as Mouser led him through the trees.

The park was home to many birds, from large ones like the heron that lived over on the banks of the lake, to the smaller wrens, robins and sparrows that nested in the woodland and drew Mouser's gaze.

Although he was very hungry, the puppy wasn't interested in the birds like Mouser was, but as soon as he saw a squirrel jump from one branch to the next he started to chase it, barking excitedly. The only problem was that there were so many squirrels that no sooner had he begun to chase one, he spotted another and raced off after that one instead, running round and round, this way and that.

Mouser didn't try to catch a squirrel, having learnt long ago that it was virtually impossible. She did catch a mouse though and would have shared it with the puppy had he not gone running off squirrelling.

She washed her face and paws as she waited for him to come running back to her, which he did a short while later. He panted with the effort of all that running, then rolled over on to his back in the morning sunshine and waggled his legs in the air just for the fun of it. Mouser dropped what was left of the mouse next to him.

Ivor and Thumbs had already caught three pet cats by the time they spotted Mouser and the puppy. They'd found a large brown sack to keep the cats in, which were now wriggling and miaowing.

'Here, puss,' they called to Mouser, but she took no notice as she watched the puppy race off after a new squirrel that had scampered down from a tree and was running across the grass.

Ivor and Thumbs ran towards Mouser.

'Get ready with the sack. We'll corner her.'

Thumbs held the sack open and Ivor slowly moved towards Mouser from the other side.

'Now!'

He pounced. Mouser yowled and the puppy turned and came running back. He clamped his teeth on to Ivor's trouser leg – for which he got a sharp kick that sent him flying. Thumbs grabbed Mouser and Mouser tried to get away, but Thumbs had already had more than one struggle with a cat since they'd started collecting them and, although she scratched and tried to bite him, he didn't let her go.

The little puppy tried to help his friend by barking and growling at the two boys, but it was no use. Mouser gave a yowl of protest as she was stuffed into the potato sack. She tore and bit desperately at the sacking, but she couldn't get away.

'Let's try and get the dog too,' Ivor said. 'I can always get a few coppers for it from the dog-fighting ring.'

People came from miles around to watch the dog fights.

'It's a bit small, isn't it?' Thumbs said.

But Ivor shook his head. 'If the dog's big enough, they'll use it in the ring – but a small one'll be used as a bait dog for the fighting dogs to practise on.'

'Doesn't look like he'd last long against a fighting dog,' Thumbs said.

The puppy was still growling, but neither of them were feeling the least bit scared.

Ivor shrugged. 'Fighting dogs have got to have something to work on. Here, dog,' he said, nodding to Thumbs to come at it from the other side. But the puppy raced away and hid in a bush before they could get close.

'Not worth following it,' Ivor said. 'Wouldn't get much for such a little scrap anyway.'

'What are we going to do with the cats now we've caught them?' Thumbs asked.

Ivor wasn't sure. But he knew where the men who wanted to join up to go to war went –

Battersea Recruiting Depot. So that is where they headed.

'You've got what in there?' the sergeant said, looking at the two scratched boys and the wriggling sack one of them was holding.

'Cats,' Ivor said. 'Four of them.'

'Cats!' the sergeant bellowed. 'What in the King's name are you bringing me cats for?'

'There's a poster by the station,' Thumbs explained patiently. 'Said cats were needed at the front. So we've brought you some.'

'Which we'll gladly hand over – for a price,' Ivor added.

The sergeant bellowed with laughter.

'You want me to pay for some stray cats!'

'They're not stra–' Thumbs started to say, but stopped when he got a sharp kick on the ankle from Ivor. 'Ouch, what did you do that for?'

'The army pays for the horses it requisitions,' Ivor said.

'Well, horses aren't cats, are they? A horse is a noble beast born to carry man into battle. Don't see many soldiers riding cats, do you? And just where did you find those cats anyway?' the sergeant asked suspiciously.

'Never mind,' Ivor sighed. He nodded to Thumbs to pick up the sack. They'd just have to let the cats go.

'Wait!' the sergeant bellowed as they reached the door.

Ivor looked round hopefully. Maybe he'd changed his mind and was going to pay for the cats after all.

'I think you can leave them here,' the sergeant said. 'Unless you want to explain again where you got them from?'

Ivor rolled his eyes as Thumbs put the sack down. They'd have to think of another way to make some money. But it was going to be hard to beat the shilling a day the army paid its privates.

Chapter 4

The puppy ran back along the alley behind the Jensons' house as fast as his little legs would go. Perhaps he'd find his friend there.

When he arrived at the house, he tried to jump over the back garden fence like he'd seen Mouser do, but it wasn't as easy for him. He tried again and again without managing it. It was really too high for a puppy to jump over, but he wouldn't give up. He trotted up the alley a little way and then turned and ran back at the fence. This time he almost made it, but not quite; he had to scrabble with his claws clinging to the top to get over it, and he fell into the garden head first with a yelp. A moment later he was up and barking at the kitchen door.

Lizzie and Arthur had just arrived home from school.

'It's a puppy,' Lizzie said in surprise as she looked out. Arthur came to see too.

'I think it's the same dog that went off with Mouser along the alley this morning,' Arthur said. 'Oliver and I saw him, but only from quite far away.'

He opened the kitchen door and the puppy came running in and then almost immediately hopped back out again. He looked behind him at Lizzie and Arthur and whined.

'You don't think something's happened to Mouser, do you?' Lizzie said. She couldn't think what the puppy could be doing here. Didn't it have an owner?

'I think he wants us to go with him,' Arthur

said, and they went out into the garden and opened the back gate.

The puppy ran on ahead of them, checking every now and again that they were still behind him, occasionally barking or whining. Why didn't the children hurry up?

'He's limping,' Lizzie said.

'I hope he wasn't hit by a car,' Arthur said.

They glanced at each other, both of them worrying that Mouser might have been knocked over; cars travelled so much faster than a horse and cart.

'There's very few cars about, so it's unlikely,' Arthur told her.

'But Mouser might not realize she could get hurt by one; she's probably never even seen one,' Lizzie said, putting into words what Arthur was thinking.

'And, knowing Mouser, she'd probably think she could take on a car and win,' said Arthur.

Lizzie smiled because that did sound like

their fearless Mouser, but she couldn't bear the idea she might have got hurt too.

'Oh, I do hope she's OK,' she said. 'Maybe we should ask that boy if he's seen her.'

Ivor was leaning on a lamp post just outside the park entrance ahead of them. Although Lizzie didn't really know him, she'd seen him playing football with Oliver before.

'That's Ivor,' Arthur hissed. 'He's not very nice.'

Thumbs had gone home for his dinner and Ivor was feeling bitter at not being paid for the cats they'd caught. When he saw the puppy, he pulled a bit of string from his pocket and, quick as a flash, he put a noose round its neck.

'What are you doing?' Lizzie asked, outraged.

'I see you found my dog.' He grinned gummily at Lizzie and Arthur. 'Been looking for him everywhere, I have.'

Lizzie stared in horror at the bit of dirty string now tied tightly round the little puppy's neck. The puppy wriggled and tugged and jumped about, making little yelping sounds.

'It doesn't look like he recognizes you,' said Lizzie.

'Come on, puppy,' Ivor said as he dragged the little dog off. 'He loves pretend playing – trying to get away,' he said over his shoulder to Lizzie.

Lizzie bit her bottom lip as she looked at Arthur. He seemed just as horrified as she was. He knew Ivor a little bit from the football games he sometimes joined in, but he'd never really talked to him and had always tried to avoid him whenever he could. They were both sure the puppy couldn't really belong to Ivor – but then they both knew it didn't belong to them either.

'Ger' on with ya,' Ivor growled, and kicked out at the puppy as it tried to nip his trouser leg.

As Ivor struggled to drag the puppy along with him, Lizzie and Arthur followed them, unsure what to do. In the end Ivor was almost carrying the puppy by the rope around its neck, the dog's little feet scrabbling in the air.

'He'll kill it, holding it like that,' Lizzie said, and she and Arthur were about to call out when a young apple-cheeked woman, much shorter and rounder than either of the two children, came out of a large building opposite them and saw Ivor with the dog. Her mouth tightened and she put her hands on her hips.

'I see you've found another dog, Ivor,' she called out to him.

'What's it to you?' Ivor shouted back. ''S my dog and I can do what I like with it.'

'If it's your dog then pray tell what its name is?' she asked.

'Er . . .' Ivor tried flashing his gummy smile as he looked past her.

He wasn't frightened of the two children, or the little round woman. But he could see lots of other ladies coming out of the large building behind her and they were starting to look at him too. *Interfering busybodies,* he thought. But he decided to change his tune.

'Poor little thing must've got himself lost.'

'Well then, I suggest you take him to the Dogs Home; it's just around the corner after all. We'll come with you, to make sure he arrives safe and sound,' the young woman said.

'Are you one of those suffer-suffragettes?' Lizzie asked her as they all hurried down the road. She'd never met one before, but she recognized the rosette with the green, white and purple colours that the lady was wearing on her lapel.

'Yes, I am,' the woman said, 'as well as being a nurse and an animal lover.' She nodded at the little dog who was still squirming in Ivor's arms.

'My name's Amelia Davis. Do you know what the suffragettes are, young man?' she asked Arthur.

Arthur shook his head, already a bit scared of her.

'We're women who fight for the rights of women. And do you know what our motto is?'

Arthur didn't, but that didn't matter because she didn't wait for him to answer.

'*Deeds not words*,' she said.

Arthur didn't say another word all the way to Battersea Dogs Home, which was near the railway station and bordered by the main tracks from Victoria. He had often wondered what went on at the home when he passed it.

As they reached the gates, Ivor suddenly stopped and said: 'Oh, look at the time. I forgot I have a very important appointment I can't be late for. Here, miss, you take him in.' Then he thrust the struggling puppy into a surprised Lizzie's arms. She could feel his little heart beating very fast.

He's terrified, she thought as she held him close and stroked him. 'It's all right, you're going to be all right now,' she said gently.

Amelia pursed her lips as she watched Ivor

run off and then she banged on the Dogs Home gate.

'This is my brother Kenneth,' Amelia told Lizzie and Arthur, when a man leaning on a walking stick opened it a few minutes later. Kenneth was less round and a little taller than Amelia. He had a dark bushy beard and kind brown eyes that were very much like Amelia's eyes. 'He'll know what to do.'

'Mellie.' Kenneth grinned as he tried unsuccessfully to brush the many dog hairs from his jacket.

Lizzie smiled at the nickname the man had for the rather stern-looking lady called Amelia.

'Come on in.'

Chapter 5

Lizzie and Arthur had never been through the gates of the home for lost and starving dogs before, although everyone in the area knew of it, and they hadn't realized just how big it was. Five railway arches were used as dog kennels and there were other buildings on the site as well as land to exercise the dogs on.

'Battersea hasn't seen fit to employ women – yet,' Amelia said, giving Kenneth a stern look, but speaking to Lizzie and Arthur, 'although it was founded by one. It doesn't turn its nose up at female volunteers though.'

'Now then, Mellie,' Kenneth said. 'Don't you go getting on your high horse. Who's this little chap?'

'We don't know his name,' Lizzie told him.

'He and our cat, Mouser, went off together this morning,' Arthur added. 'They're friends. But now we don't know where our cat is.'

'Cats are quite able to take care of themselves, in my experience,' Amelia said. 'I'm sure it'll come home when it's hungry.'

'Cat and dog friends, that's unusual,' Kenneth said. 'Usually cats are a bit wary of dogs, and with good reason.'

'You haven't met our cat. She's not afraid of anything,' Arthur grinned. He was proud of Mouser.

'We think this puppy came to tell us something was wrong,' Lizzie said quietly, although now, even as she said the words, she thought how silly they sounded. It was just a puppy after all.

'He jumped over our back fence and barked at the kitchen door,' Arthur added.

Kenneth took the puppy from Lizzie and he whimpered and looked back at her.

'We think he's hurt,' Arthur said.

'He was limping,' said Lizzie.

'Trembling like a leaf, poor little lamb, but I don't think there's much wrong with his leg. Have to be careful with puppies though. This one can't be more than six or seven months old.'

'He'd have been worse than trembling if he'd ended up in the dog-fighting ring that I think that young man, Ivor Dawson, was heading for,' Amelia said. 'Wouldn't have stood a chance, the poor wee thing. I'm sure the patients at my hospital would love him though. I wish they could meet him.'

'Ivor told us the puppy was his at first,' Lizzie told Kenneth, and Amelia rolled her eyes.

'A highly unlikely story,' she said.

The little dog whimpered.

'Don't you worry, I'll keep an eye on him,' Kenneth told them. 'But he'll need a name. Do you two want to do the honours as you're the ones that saved him?'

Lizzie smiled and whispered to Arthur. They'd often talked about what they would call a dog if their mother ever let them have one, which they both knew was extremely unlikely.

'Sammy,' they both said. 'We want to call him Sammy.'

'Suits him.' Kenneth smiled.

The puppy sniffed at Kenneth's jacket and then tried to get his head into Kenneth's pocket.

'What's he doing?' Arthur laughed.

'He's trying to get to my sandwich,' Kenneth told them. 'This little chap's hungry.'

He pulled the sandwich from his pocket and broke off a crust.

'Here you go then.'

Sammy gobbled it up as Amelia hurried away and came back with a bowl of chopped meat and biscuits. Kenneth put the puppy down and he ran to the food and began gulping it down.

'Slow down there now, Sammy, or you'll make yourself sick,' Kenneth said.

But the puppy had already finished almost all of the food and was licking the bowl clean to make sure there wasn't even the tiniest bit left.

'He was very hungry,' Lizzie said.

'Almost starving, I'd say,' said Kenneth. 'It's lucky for him he ended up here.'

'Very lucky indeed,' Amelia said as Sammy drank from the water bowl.

For the first time since they arrived, Lizzie realized she could hear lots of other dogs, big and small. Some of them were barking, others whining. One was making a howl that sounded almost like he was crying.

'That's Toby,' Kenneth said as he noticed Lizzie looking around. 'He's been making that noise since he arrived here three days ago. Pining to go home, I think, poor thing.'

'Will he get to go home?' Arthur asked him.

Kenneth shook his head. 'Probably not. The police brought him in when they found him wandering the streets. Looked like he might have been hit by a vehicle of some sort. Toby's not his real name, but we have to call him something.'

'What sort of dog is he?'

'A tan-coated, slobbery summer dog.'

'What's a *summer* dog?' asked Arthur.

'It's a term people use for mixed-breed dogs, as in *summer this* and *summer that*,' explained Kenneth, which made Arthur smile.

'How many dogs do get to go home?' Lizzie said.

Kenneth frowned. 'Hard to say exactly, but not enough, that's for sure. Some of our long-term resident dogs have gone to help with the war effort. The army came to us first when they needed them. The men that work here couldn't wait to join up too. There used to be thirty of us kennelmen up until a month ago, but ten have enlisted so far and it looks like more will be going soon, so we need as much help as we can get.'

'We'll help,' Arthur said, and Lizzie agreed.

'Much appreciated,' Kenneth told them. 'I'd join up myself but for this.' He tapped at his right leg with his walking stick. 'Had an accident when I was a boy.'

'Fell out of a tree,' Amelia said, 'trying to rescue a cat and broke his leg.'

'Never set right,' Kenneth told them.

'Cat was fine,' Amelia added. 'Got itself out of the tree without any help and ran off home.'

'Told them I was fit to fight, but they showed me the door,' Kenneth said, shaking his head.

'Good thing too, you're needed here,' Amelia told him.

The talk about cats made Arthur wonder if maybe Mouser had been handed in.

'Have you had any grey tabby cats brought in today?' he asked.

Kenneth wasn't sure. 'But we can go and ask,' he said.

He found a collar and lead for Sammy and, once he'd put them on him, he gave the lead to Lizzie. Sammy looked up at her and wagged his tail as they all headed over to the cat area.

The cats were housed in a separate building to the dogs, but they had to pass the dogs' kennels to get to it. When they went into the cat area, it seemed to be a lot calmer with a lot less noise than had been coming from the dogs' kennels.

Sammy looked in at the different cats as they

went past their cages, but although some of them looked a bit like Mouser none of them were her.

Most of the cats weren't as keen to be friends with Sammy as he was to be friends with them. They hissed or headed over to the back of their cages when they saw him coming.

Nevertheless, Sammy gave a hopeful half-wag of his tail at some of the cages and was very interested in the different cat smells around him.

'How long have you had cats at the home?' Arthur asked Kenneth.

'Almost as long as the dogs have been here. There were seven hundred and eighty-seven in 1907 – the year I started working here,' Kenneth told them. 'Don't know exactly how many there are now. But some of them will be going to France and Belgium to become trench cats soon.'

'We thought that was just a rumour. Do they

really have cats at the front? Why do they need trench cats?' Lizzie asked.

'Because of the rats,' Kenneth told her. 'And as an early warning if there's a poison gas attack, of course.'

'Shh, Kenneth,' Amelia said, looking at Lizzie and Arthur's stricken faces. 'There won't be any poison gas attacks.'

'No,' Kenneth quickly agreed. 'But if there was one the cats and dogs, being so much smaller than the soldiers, would feel the effects of it first and it'd give the soldiers time to react.'

'Like canaries in mines,' Arthur said slowly. 'As long as the birds keep singing, the miners know they're safe.'

'Quite,' said Amelia brusquely. 'Now are any of these cats yours?'

Lizzie shook her head.

Although quite a few of the cats were grey as well as ginger, tabby, black-and-white, white and Siamese, none of them was Mouser.

'Do you want to have a look round the rest of the home and see where your pup'll be sleeping?' Kenneth asked Lizzie and Arthur, hoping it might distract them from their missing cat.

'Yes, please,' they said, and they headed away from the cats and kittens to the kennels for the dogs. Before Kenneth had even reached the door to open it, there was a cacophony of barks from inside.

'One starts and then they all do,' he said.

Sammy cowered away, ducking behind Lizzie's legs. 'It's all right,' Lizzie told him. 'They won't hurt you.'

As they passed each of the dog's cages, the dogs inside them hurried to the cage gate, barking and whining and wagging their tails winningly. Some even put their paws out.

'That's Toby,' Kenneth said as a large tan-coated, mixed-breed dog hurried over to them, making the whining sound they'd heard earlier.

61

Lizzie swallowed hard at the obvious desperation of some of the dogs. It was so sad seeing them in cages like this. There was every type of dog she could imagine and some that she hadn't even thought of. They should be in homes being loved and cared for, she thought, like Mouser. She hoped Amelia was right and that Mouser would come home when she was hungry. Mouser had gone off before, once even for a few days, but she'd always come home, so Lizzie thought it probably wasn't time to panic.

'Some of the dogs do get to go home or are rehomed somewhere new,' Kenneth said as if he were reading Lizzie's thoughts. 'Although not as many as I'd like. We had another summer dog – quirky-looking thing – that went home a week ago. I'll never forget how happy he was to see his owner. As he got to the gates, he turned back, looked straight at me and barked.'

'Just like he was saying thank you,' said

Amelia, who'd heard the story a few times already, and winked at Lizzie and Arthur.

'And then do you know what he did?' Kenneth said.

Arthur shook his head.

Kenneth's eyes turned misty at the memory. 'He ran back and licked my hand.'

Sammy looked up at Kenneth as if he were listening to the story too.

'Some of the medium and larger dogs are going to help with the war effort, aren't they, Kenneth?' Amelia said pointedly.

'What'll they have to do?' Arthur asked.

'Guard the soldiers and their ammunition and warn them if the enemy approaches,' Kenneth told him.

'I don't like dogs having to go to war,' said Lizzie.

'Me neither,' said Kenneth. 'But they've used dogs in wars for as long as there's been wars – and that's a long, long time.'

They walked on through the kennels and, wherever they went, dogs looked at them with pleading eyes.

'Do you get two dogs from the same family sometimes?'

Kenneth nodded. 'And we've had more than one case when a pregnant dog's been brought in and her pups have been born here.'

'Puppies are so sweet,' Lizzie said, looking down at Sammy.

'But it's hard for them to survive on their own,' Kenneth said. 'Since the start of the war more and more dogs are being abandoned. I've had some owners, desperate owners, take off their dog's collar, put a bit of string round the dog's neck instead, like your puppy had, and bring it here, claiming it's a stray, when it was clearly a family pet. Breaks your heart to see.'

'Breaks the dog's heart too, no doubt,' Amelia added softly.

They came to an empty cage with a bowl

of water in one corner and a blanket at the back.

'This one's free,' Kenneth said as he opened the door.

Lizzie let go of the lead and Sammy ran in and started to drink the water. Kenneth closed the door and bolted it.

Sammy stopped drinking and raced to the cage door. He didn't want to be shut in. He wanted to go with Lizzie and Arthur. But he wasn't quick enough to get out. He barked his high puppy bark and all of them heard and turned back. But they didn't have a choice.

'We could ask our mum,' Lizzie said doubtfully. 'But I don't think we'll be allowed to keep him.' In her heart she knew they wouldn't.

'Can we come back one morning before school?' Arthur asked Kenneth as Sammy pushed his little paw through the bars of the cage. 'To see how he's getting on?'

'Yes, you'd be more than welcome. And maybe you could do a bit of cat socializing while you're here, as you're used to cats.'

'What's cat socializing?' Arthur asked.

'Cats, even pet cats like your Mouser, need to be regularly stroked or they won't let anyone touch them. It's like they turn back into their wild-cat selves and, if they do that, no one will want to adopt them or be able to do anything with them. Plus, there's the cage guarding – when cats are confined to a small space, they can become stressed and territorial.'

'We'll help socialize them,' Lizzie and Arthur promised. 'We'd like to do it.'

Amelia left the Dogs Home with them. 'My shift at the hospital starts in twenty minutes,' she said. 'But I always like to look in on the dogs and cats when I can. Hope to see you there again soon. They could really do with volunteers.'

'We'll be there,' Arthur and Lizzie promised. 'We won't let them down.'

'Give your cat a stroke from me when she comes home,' Amelia said as she turned the corner to go to the hospital.

'We will.'

Chapter 6

Mouser hadn't had any breakfast and she didn't get any supper either. She hadn't liked being bounced around in the rough sack with the other cats and now she didn't like being shut in a cage that rocked horribly back and forth.

There were three other cats in the cage with her: two black-and-white moggies and a ginger one with a white tip to its tail. Whenever they came close, Mouser hissed and spat at them. The other cats now sat huddled together in the corner at the back of the cage, giving Mouser a wide berth.

Mouser miaowed loudly through the bars of the cage as two men approached.

'Shall I feed them, Captain?' one of the men asked.

'No point,' the other answered. 'Don't want them to be too full up to bother to chase the rats, do we? Hungry cats make the best ratters and there'll be plenty of rats for them to eat once they're at the front. Might even be a few to catch on this boat in the meantime . . .' he said thoughtfully.

'There's more than enough at the front!' a soldier, sitting on his kitbag in the corner, chimed in. 'It's like rat paradise over there. Never seen so many or such big ones.' He shuddered at the memory. 'They're not frightened of people any more, I tell you. Many a soldier's woken up to find a large furry rat snuggled right up beside him.'

The more cats they had out there the better as far as he was concerned. They could never have too many.

The captain of the boat peered into the cat cage.

'Fine-looking cat that one,' he said, pointing at Mouser as he stroked his beard. 'Fine-looking cat indeed. Just the sort of cat a captain of a boat like this might choose to have permanently onboard.'

'These cats are for the front,' the soldier who'd brought them aboard said firmly.

'But surely they can spare one,' the captain replied. He was doing them a favour ferrying the cats over to France. There wasn't anything about being a cat transporter in his orders. 'It isn't like boats and ships don't have rats too, you know. Rats get everywhere.'

He put his finger through the wire of the cage to stroke Mouser. But instead of purring, as he'd expected her to do, she hissed and swiped at him with her claws so he quickly took his finger back out.

'On reflection, I don't think we do need a cat on board after all,' he said.

The soldier who'd been at the front grinned.

'That cat'll show those rats what for,' he said, and the other man agreed.

Chapter 7

By the time Mouser set off, Oliver, Patrick and the rest of the Battersea Beasts PALs battalion had already reached the thin strip of land between Germany, France and Belgium that was known as the Western Front.

The first job they had to do was help dig more trenches and reinforce those that had already been made. They got there by marching along a communication trench that connected the different trenches together and was used for taking messages and supplies.

'This is going to become your second home,

lads,' Sergeant Wainwright said as the shovels were handed out. 'So you might as well make yourselves comfortable. Or at least as comfortable as you can. Those German soldiers want to secure the seaports, go right through Belgium and take Paris in a swift victory. But we're not going to let that happen, are we?'

'No, Sarge,' the men said.

'Your time here'll be divided between three trench lines: the front trench line which is closest to the enemy's trenches so it's the most dangerous; this one, which is about eighty yards behind the front line, known as the support trench line; and the reserve trench line which is another three hundred yards behind us. Oh, and if you're very lucky you might get a bit of leave and won't need to be in a trench at all.'

'How long will we be in the front line for, Sarge?' Patrick asked. He'd heard a rumour that in the front line trench not only did you have to face the enemy, but sometimes soldiers had to stand for days in muddy water. He wasn't looking forward to it.

'Four days in each trench line – usually,' the sergeant told him. 'But nothing's fixed in stone in a war, son. Eight or more days isn't that unusual.'

'But it'll all be over by Christmas, won't it?' Patrick asked as the Battersea Beasts set to work digging in the support trench.

'If we do our jobs right it should. So get digging!' the sergeant bellowed.

It was awkward digging in such a confined space, but they did the best they could.

'You'll be digging in your sleep soon, lads,' the sergeant told them as he inspected their work, sounding overly jolly. 'If you can get any sleep, that is. Make sure you keep your head down as you dig. Don't want to get it shot at by an enemy sniper, do you?'

Oliver kept his head down from then on, although it was very tempting to try to see what was on the other side of the trench.

'The trenches need to be no more than seven feet deep and six feet wide, following a zigzag pattern,' the sergeant explained.

'Why can't they be straight, Sarge?' one of the new soldiers asked. 'It'd be a lot simpler.'

The sergeant held up his rifle and pretended to take aim at the men who'd been digging, but now straightened their backs to hear his answer.

'If I shot this gun from here at you lot, just think about the damage I could do. You'd all be like sitting ducks. I couldn't miss. But my gun doesn't shoot in zigzags and a gas attack won't spread as far either. The reason you're digging like this is so you get a chance to go home and see your mothers one day.'

'Right, sir,' the soldier said, thinking about what he'd said.

They all got back to digging and didn't moan

too much about their aching backs and blistered hands.

'Stand back!' the sergeant yelled suddenly. Oliver dropped his shovel and stepped back in surprise as a collie dog came racing down the tunnel towards them, its face steady in concentration and a tin canister attached to its collar.

Oliver reached out to the dog. It seemed so desperate to him. But one of the more experienced soldiers, who'd been at the front almost since the start of the war and the Boer War before that, grabbed Oliver's arm and pulled him back as he was about to touch it and the dog ran past.

'Didn't you listen in your training when they said it's a court-martial offence to stop a messenger dog from doing his duty?' the grizzled-looking soldier hissed.

'What? No,' Oliver said. 'I was only going to stroke it.'

The soldier shook his head. 'You and just about every other Tommy soldier, and the problem's not just that too many soldiers have been stroking and making a fuss of them. They've been feeding them as well. It distracts the dogs and stops them from doing their job.'

'That, lads,' said the sergeant, who fortunately hadn't seen Oliver trying to stroke the dog, 'was a messenger dog, a French messenger dog by the look of it. We don't have any of our own here yet. But now we've seen what they can do we're hoping to get some trained up.'

'Do the Germans have messenger dogs, Sarge?' one of the Battersea Beasts asked.

'Yes, they do. In fact, I'm told that every German army headquarters on the Western Front has a messenger dog section attached to it called a *Meldehundstaffel.*'

'Why don't we have them?' Oliver asked.

'We will, lad. Once we get our act together. But in the meantime we need some volunteer human messenger dogs – or dispatch runners. Any of you lot good at running? Your mates' lives might depend on you getting that message through and you'll need to be fast. Gas attacks, not that we've had any yet, and German raids wait for no man.'

'I'll do it, sir,' Oliver said.

'And are you fast? Have you got stamina?' the sergeant asked him.

'You should see him on the football pitch,' the other Battersea Beasts told the sergeant as Oliver grinned. 'Then you'd know.'

'Right, any more volunteers?'

Patrick volunteered too as did some of the others.

'Looks like most of you reckon you could be dispatch runners. Come on then, let's see what you've got.'

Running between the three main trench

lines were communication trenches that enabled soldiers and supplies to be moved from one line to another without being exposed to enemy snipers. A few miles further back, past the reserve trench, was HQ and the artillery supplies.

Sergeant Wainwright led the lads to the communication trench and pointed down it. 'I want you to run down there, past the reserve trench to HQ and back again. Three-mile round trip.'

Oliver and the other volunteers lined up, all eager to show what they could do. The sergeant looked at his military-issue pocket watch.

'Wait for the second hand to get to the twelve. Ready, set, go!'

Oliver ran as fast as he could, gradually pulling ahead of all the others. By the time he passed the reserve trench, he'd taken the lead, although there wasn't much between him and Patrick when they reached the deserted farm where HQ was based, a mile or so further on, and turned to come back.

Oliver dashed over the finish first with Patrick just inches behind him.

The sergeant looked at his pocket watch. 'Sixteen minutes. Right, you've definitely got what it takes,' he said to Oliver. 'And you as reserve,' he told Patrick. 'And the rest of you – as and when. You two, a word, please. The rest of you, there's a few hundred miles of trench to be dug.

'Being a dispatch runner is a vital role,' Sergeant Wainwright told Oliver and Patrick. 'You'll need to keep yourselves fit, so that when you're needed to take messages from the command staff at the rear to the fighting units near the battlefield you'll be ready.'

'We will, Sarge,' Oliver said, and Patrick nodded.

'What kind of messages might we be taking, Sarge?' Patrick asked.

'Most of them will be routine – lists of stores needed from the brigade – but a few might warn of an enemy attack. Fewer still . . .' The sergeant took a breath. 'And there haven't been any of these yet, thank goodness, might be to warn of a gas attack. If you're given one of those, you must run with it like your life depends on it, because it does – along with the lives of all your mates. Don't waste time trying to find me or one of the other officers, just bang on the nearest gas gong as loudly as you can.'

'What's a gas gong?' Oliver asked.

The sergeant pointed to an empty shell casing attached to a length of wire that swung down near the periscope.

'You'll find them all the way down the line. With men trapped in the trenches, poison gas can't be seen or smelt until it's often too late. Your warning will probably be all that can save them in time.'

Chapter 8

Sammy's bowl of food lay untouched beside him in his cage.

'I know it's hard being in a new place, but it's really not too bad here,' Kenneth said from the other side of the bars.

Sammy didn't even seem to hear him as he lay there with his head on his paws, looking utterly miserable. Kenneth sighed. He didn't want to leave the sad puppy, but he had to get on with his early-morning rounds. Sammy was just one of many unwanted pets that needed his attention.

Suddenly Sammy's tail started thumping on the floor of his cage. He jumped up and whined, and then barked as he looked towards the entrance door. The other dogs started to bark too and Kenneth turned to see what was happening.

'Morning.' Lizzie smiled as she came in, followed by Arthur. Sammy's tail wagged as fast as it possibly could. He stood up on his back legs with his front paws resting on the bars of his cage.

'We're not too early, are we?' Arthur said. It was just after seven thirty. 'We wanted to make sure we had enough time to spend with the animals before school.'

'Not at all,' Kenneth told them. 'Sammy's just about over the moon and back now that you're here.'

'Did you miss us?' Lizzie asked Sammy as she crouched down. It had only been a few days, but Lizzie and Arthur had certainly missed him.

Sammy made a sound somewhere between a whine and a bark. He was very excited to see his friends again.

'He's trying to talk,' Arthur said, grinning.

Lizzie noticed the puppy's full bowl of untouched food and now Sammy remembered it too. He put his head down and for the next few moments all that could be heard was the sound of his teeth crunching up his biscuits.

Once his food was all gone, he looked up at Lizzie and Arthur with his head cocked to one side.

'Now he looks like he's asking what next?' Arthur said.

'He does indeed,' Kenneth agreed as he pulled back the bolt of Sammy's cage. 'You can take him out if you like,' he said, handing Arthur Sammy's lead.

'Come on, Sammy,' Arthur said as he clipped it to the puppy's collar.

They headed out of the kennel block as the other dogs barked and whined, saying as clearly as they could that they'd like to come too. But Lizzie and Arthur could only take one dog at a time.

Kenneth watched them go. It was plain to see that Sammy felt a lot happier as he almost danced along with the children.

'Where shall we go?' Arthur asked.

'How about the park?' Lizzie said. 'It's just around the corner, and perhaps we'll see Mouser there.' Mouser still hadn't come home and Lizzie was trying not to worry.

Sammy was very well behaved on his lead and didn't pull at all as they went down the street.

'He's so well trained,' Lizzie said.

'But how did he end up getting lost? Do you think someone's looking for him?' Arthur asked.

Lizzie didn't know, but she thought she'd be beside herself with worry if she'd lost him.

'Do you think Mouser's all right?' Arthur said.

'Mum said she was probably being treated like the cat that got the cream somewhere and would come home when she's ready,' Lizzie told him.

Arthur grinned. 'Mouser is a canny cat. It's hard to imagine she'd ever be in trouble.'

Almost as soon as they walked through the park gates and let Sammy off his lead, he raced off, barking with excitement.

'Oh look, he's seen that football,' said Arthur as Sammy raced towards the ball.

Arthur and Lizzie looked at each other in surprise and then laughed.

'Well, I didn't expect that!'

'It's almost as big as him.'

Sammy didn't bite the ball, but pushed it along as he ran behind it, barking happily. It was like he'd found an old friend.

'What's he doing?' Arthur said as they ran after him.

'Looks like he's playing football!'

'I wish Oliver could see this. He'd never believe it.'

'I think he's played with one before,' Arthur said.

'Certainly seems like it,' said Lizzie.

But, although Arthur and Lizzie thought Sammy playing with the football was funny, the boy whom the ball belonged to didn't think so.

'Your dog's biting my new ball,' he said. 'He'll ruin it before I've had a chance to show it to my friends at school.'

Lizzie hadn't seen Sammy try to bite the ball once, but she knew the ball didn't belong to the puppy, however much he might want it to.

'I'm sorry,' she said. 'We'll get it back for you.'

She ran over to the ball, but Sammy thought this was all part of the game and ran off with it. Arthur tried to help by running towards the ball too – which only made the game even better from Sammy's point of view. Plus, there was the new boy shouting and waving his arms about.

Sammy swerved with the ball one way and then he ran with it the other as Lizzie and Arthur tried unsuccessfully to catch him. And all the time his tail wagged like mad because he was having so much fun.

'Sammy, give me the ball!' Lizzie shouted as she ran towards him, but Sammy didn't think that was a good idea and he ran on towards the pond. Arthur followed him and did a flying tackle to try to get the ball back. His fingers touched it for a moment, but then Sammy got it back before Lizzie came in for a tackle too. Then Arthur managed to snatch the ball and held it above his head while Sammy barked and tried to jump up and get it.

'Sorry, Sammy, but it's not yours,' Arthur

said as the other boy came running over and took the ball from him.

Sammy went to run after it, but Lizzie said, 'No.' And Sammy stopped and looked back at her. He wagged his tail, unsure, then looked back at the ball, which he really wanted to play with.

Arthur picked up a stick and waggled it in front of him. 'Here, Sammy, look, what's this?' he said, and he threw the stick as far as he could. 'Fetch it, fetch,' he said, pointing at where the stick had landed. Sammy just gave him a look. He had no intention of chasing a stick. He looked over to where the boy with the ball was heading off into the distance and whined.

'We know you want to play with the ball,' Lizzie said, 'but it isn't ours.'

Arthur picked up another stick. 'Come on, Sammy,' he said. 'Chasing a stick can be just as much fun as chasing a ball.' He threw the stick and then ran after it himself while trying to encourage Sammy to copy him. 'Come on, Sammy, this way, this way.'

'Like this, Sammy,' Lizzie said, and she chased after the stick too.

Sammy went with them, but he had none of the same enthusiasm for the stick that he'd had for the ball. The sky darkened and there was a rumble of thunder in the distance. Sammy heard it and started to tremble.

'What's wrong with him?' Arthur said.

Lizzie didn't know. 'We'd better take him back,' she said.

They hurried back to the Dogs Home, both worried that something was seriously wrong with him.

'Have a nice time?' Kenneth asked them when they got back. Amelia was with him.

'We did. Sammy found a football and he loved playing with it only –' Lizzie started to say when suddenly there was a flash of lightning outside and Sammy whimpered with fear. He crouched down and covered his face with his paws.

'It's the storm. Lots of pets don't like thunder and lightning. You just hold him and tell him it's all going to be fine. That's it now,' Amelia said as Lizzie bent down and cuddled the puppy to her.

'It's OK,' Arthur told him as he stroked Sammy's head. 'There's nothing to be frightened of.'

The rumble came again and now Sammy was panting as well as trembling. He gave a little whine that was almost like a cry.

'He sounds just like some of my patients,' Amelia said, shaking her head. She'd popped in for a quick cup of tea on her way to work. 'Simply terrified. More and more badly wounded soldiers are arriving back from the front every day. Many of them are reliving the horrors of what they've seen . . .'

Kenneth gave his sister a look. There was

no need to worry Lizzie and Arthur. He knew their friend Oliver was at the front.

But Amelia didn't notice his glare. 'I really think that if the hospital would just allow me to take in the calmest of the dogs and cats, and let the traumatized soldiers stroke them and spend time with them, it'd really help,' she said. So far she hadn't been given permission to do so, but she wasn't giving up.

'I think that's a great idea,' said Lizzie. 'I know whenever I'm sad that stroking Mouser always makes me feel better.'

Lizzie and Arthur stayed with Sammy until the storm had almost passed, but then Lizzie remembered her promise to her mother – they could volunteer at the Dogs Home so long as they didn't miss any school.

'Come on, Arthur, we're going to be late!'

Before the war, boys and girls over the age of ten had been taught in separate buildings at the school. But so many teachers had joined up and gone off to fight in the war that all the children were now taught together.

'You're late!' Miss Hailstock said when Arthur and Lizzie ran into the classroom, breathless.

'We're sorry, miss,' Arthur said, and he and Lizzie told their teacher about volunteering at the Dogs Home.

'Some of the dogs and cats are being sent off to help with the war,' Lizzie explained.

Miss Hailstock's fiancé and her brother and her father were already at the front.

'Well, just make sure you're not late again,' she told Lizzie and Arthur as they hurriedly took their seats on the long wooden bench.

Chapter 9

Mouser had been bumping around in the cage at the back of the horse-drawn cart for far too long. The muddy lanes the overloaded horse clipped down were uneven and the cage was bouncing around, flinging the cats together.

'Whoa there!' the driver shouted every time the horse stumbled, before urging it onwards again.

The trundling horse ride felt much worse than the slow rocking she'd got used to on the boat. Every so often the cart stopped and soldiers got off it and supplies were removed.

Occasionally the cage door opened and a hand reached inside. Mouser made sure she backed as far into the corner as she could, far away from the large hand that reached in to grab one of her companions.

The ginger cat went first and then the other two moggies. Once Mouser was left in the cage by herself, she claimed it completely as her own and hissed and spat any time a hand came near.

Hours and hours later the cart stopped dead with a final jerk and jolt. Mouser crouched low in the cage, alert and watchful.

'Is this cat for here?' a soldier's voice asked the cart driver as the last of the supplies were passed down and a large bucket of water was brought for the carthorse to drink from.

'Yes – take the cage down the communication trench, would you?' The driver looked at his orders. 'Cat's to go to the front-line trench.'

Mouser hissed at the soldier as he lifted her cage out of the cart.

'Don't put your fingers too close,' the driver warned as the soldier carried Mouser's cage into a muddy tunnel.

The cage bumped far worse than it had done on the back of the horse-drawn cart as the soldier carried it. Every now and again he'd groan with the effort of carrying the awkward cage.

'It'd be much easier if I could just let you out,' he told Mouser.

Mouser snarled at him.

The soldier put the cage down with a bump when they reached their destination.

'Not one I'll be missing,' he said.

'Oh, thank goodness. If there's one thing we need here, it's a cat to keep the rats down,' said the young officer when he saw Mouser's cage behind the supplies that were being delivered. 'The trenches are full of them.'

The young officer had only been at the front for two weeks, but he'd seen far more rats than he wanted to in his whole life. 'We've tried everything from rat traps to hitting them with our shovels, but they're so fast – and so clever.' He didn't like to tell the soldier delivering the cat that last night he'd had a nightmare about a giant rat, so he was very glad to see the cat, very glad indeed. 'This cat's going to have its work cut out. Here, puss!'

The young officer slowly unlatched Mouser's cage. Mouser saw her opportunity and, quick as a flash, she was out and away.

'Stop, come back,' the desperate officer cried as he ran after her. 'You'll like it here, I promise.'

At first, the other soldiers nudged and grinned at each other as they saw the officer chasing after the moggy, but then they realized what having no cat would mean – even more rats!

'Quick! Stop it – stop the cat!'

'It's headed your way . . .'

'Try and corner it!'

'Blasted cat . . .'

'Here, puss.'

Large hands reached out to grab her, but Mouser evaded them all as she ran along the wooden duckboards that had been placed over the muddy earth floor of the trench. Soldiers ran after her, stumbling over each other as they tried to catch her. But Mouser was too fast for them.

Two burly soldiers launched themselves at her in a flying tackle. One came away with a handful of snatched muddy fur. The other grabbed for Mouser's tail as she nimbly leapt up the side of the trench and swished her tail away just in time.

'Well, we can't stop her now. I'm not going over the top to catch a cat.'

Over the top of the trench was no-man's-land and nobody wanted to go there in daylight. It was the strip of land that belonged to neither the Germans nor the Allies, but lay in between their two sets of trenches. A strip of land that was so dangerous that, if a soldier went into it and was seen by a sniper from the other side, he'd more than likely be shot. It was too risky even to put your head above the top of the trench and so they used periscopes to look across to the German trenches and the Germans did the same.

But no one shot at Mouser and she was small enough to slip under the barbed wire that surrounded the final trench to stop the enemy from getting too close.

'Fritz'll probably eat it for breakfast,' the disgruntled soldier said, and chuckled to himself. They'd heard all sorts of rumours about the nasty things the Germans, or 'Fritz' as they'd started to call them, were supposed to have done.

Once Mouser realized she was free of the hands that had tried to grab her, she slowed down and looked about her.

There were no trees like the ones that

blossomed in the park back at home, only barren trunks, if they stood at all. What little grass there was, was brown and patchy, and there weren't any birds to chase.

Mouser looked out on to the bleak landscape before her and uttered a loud miaow. She was all alone.

Chapter 10

'Right, now check on those sandbags and then join the rest of the men,' Oliver's sergeant told him and Patrick.

The sandbags were at the front of the trench, known as the parapet. Both the front and the back of the trench were protected by two to three feet of sandbags and beyond that there was barbed wire for added protection.

Oliver and Patrick stacked back up the sandbags that had fallen, while being careful not to lift their heads too high in case they were spotted by a German sniper.

'It's dangerous enough doing this here,' Patrick said. 'But I wouldn't like to be doing it with the Germans shooting at us on the front line.'

They'd been in the support line for three days and they both knew they'd be sent to the front line soon.

'Check on those duckboards too,' the sergeant yelled to them.

The wooden slatted duckboards were laid along the muddy ground of the trenches to form a dry passageway to walk over. But with everyone on them all day long they often needed replacing.

Oliver took out the two that were split and Patrick went to fetch new ones.

At dusk every night Oliver and the rest of the soldiers in the trench were ordered to climb up on to the firing step with their bayonets attached to their rifles to practise guarding against an enemy raid.

'Stand to!' Sergeant Wainwright shouted, and the soldiers stood, ready and alert.

'Stand down,' he told them, half an hour later. 'Right, lads, dinnertime next. This way.'

The soldiers lined up behind him.

'What have you got for us?' Sergeant Wainwright asked the cook.

'Maconochie All-in,' he was told.

'Lads, you're in for a treat.'

Oliver looked down at the watery stew made from vegetables and beef in his food tin.

'What's in it?' one of the soldiers said.

'What it looks like,' said someone else.

'Beef, potatoes, carrots, onions, beans, stock, flour, lard and salt,' the cook said in one breath. He was asked the same question every day.

Once night fell, there were more chores to be done under cover of darkness. Food and medical supplies needed to be taken down the communication trench to the front-line trench and the barbed wire surrounding the trenches had to be checked and repaired.

'It's not what I expected,' Patrick said as he rewound the wire.

Oliver didn't exactly know what he'd thought it would be like.

'All over by Christmas,' he said cheerfully as they went back to their trench and tried to get some sleep while sitting up.

Christmas wasn't that far away.

Chapter 11

Lizzie and Arthur ran all the way home from school to see if Mouser was waiting for them on the window sill.

'I'd let her have all my pillow to sleep on if she'd just come back,' Lizzie told Arthur.

It had been days and days since Mouser had gone and the house felt all wrong without her there.

But Mouser wasn't on the window sill or in any of her usual hiding places.

Arthur knew how worried Lizzie was about

their cat, as was he. They now went to the Dogs Home every morning before school and most days after school too to play with Sammy and to see if Mouser had been handed in, but there was no sign of her yet.

Arthur went to fetch Oliver's football. 'Come on,' he said to Lizzie. 'I'll show you how to head the ball.' He hoped it might help to take her mind off worrying about their missing cat, and he knew how much Lizzie secretly liked playing football.

She'd always avoided heading the ball before as it looked too painful, but Arthur insisted it wasn't. He threw the ball directly at her and she managed to knock it away.

'That's it.'

But as they practised the sky darkened.

'Looks like there's going to be another storm,' Arthur said.

'Sammy will be so frightened,' said Lizzie.

'I wish there was something we could do to help him. Maybe a blanket . . .'

But suddenly Arthur knew just what Sammy needed to make him forget about the storm. He looked down at the football he was holding.

'Oliver told us not to leave it on the shelf and you saw what Sammy was like with that one in the park,' he said.

Lizzie nodded her head, but she was a bit doubtful. Oliver had given them the ball to look after while he was gone. It wasn't theirs to give away.

'We're not giving it to Sammy for good,' Arthur said. 'We're just lending it to him so he can snuggle up to it when he gets frightened by the storm. But we won't let him take it with him if he goes to live somewhere else.'

'Oh, I don't want him to live anywhere else. Unless he came here, of course. I wouldn't mind if he came to live with us.'

'Nor would I,' grinned Arthur. 'I'd love it if he did, and I bet Oliver would be totally crazy about him because they both love football so much. And Mouser would like it too, once she comes back.'

'Mum would never let us adopt a stray dog though,' Lizzie said. 'Especially not with Mouser still missing.'

'She might,' Arthur said. 'Sammy is Mouser's friend after all. He might even be able to help us find her.'

They decided to ask their mother about it when she came home from work, but in the meantime they hurried back to the Dogs Home with Oliver's football.

'Hello again,' Kenneth said when he saw them. 'I thought it was only going to be once today.'

'We thought Sammy might like to borrow this,' Arthur said, showing Kenneth the football.

In the distance there was the rumble of thunder.

'He was so frightened of the storm before . . .'

'And he so liked a football he found in the park . . .'

'He could keep it,' said Lizzie, 'only it isn't really ours to give. It belongs to Oliver, our friend who's gone to war. But we think he'd be happy for Sammy to play with it.'

Sammy raced over to them and stood on his back legs with his front paws poking through the bars as soon as he saw them.

'Hello, Sammy,' Arthur said, and he crouched down and showed Sammy the ball. 'Look what we've got for you.' Sammy's tail flicked back and forth very fast. Arthur looked up at Lizzie and smiled. He knew they'd done the right thing. 'Shall we tell Kenneth we'd like to adopt him?' he whispered.

But Lizzie thought they should wait until after they'd spoken to their mother before they said anything. She might take a lot of persuading.

Chapter 12

That night Sammy fell asleep, snuggled up to his football with one paw resting on top of it.

Kenneth smiled as he looked through the bars at him. The threatening storm hadn't come to pass and Sammy, and the many other dogs and cats at the home that were frightened of thunder and lightning, were sleeping peacefully. Kenneth stood for a moment, just watching the puppy's little chest rise and fall. Then he heard the sound of someone at the gate and hurried out to see who it could be.

A soldier in uniform was standing there. He looked agitated.

'Can I help you, sir?' Kenneth asked him. 'We are closed for the night.'

'I have to come in. I need a dog. The colonel told me to get him one, but there were so many things on the list . . . I'm his adjutant and if I go back without one . . .' He raised his hands in a gesture of helplessness and gave a loud sigh. 'Well, I'll be for it.'

Kenneth noted the man's boots. Only soldiers in the cavalry wore boots.

He opened the gate. 'Hold on, son, slow down – you're not making much sense. What will you be needing this dog for?' he asked as he led the soldier towards the kennels.

'As a mascot. He, or she, will be very well treated, believe me. More than most of the men. My colonel dotes on dogs. He says a dog will be just the ticket for raising the men's spirits.'

They hadn't even reached the kennels when Toby's mournful howl tore through the air.

'What in the world is that?' the cavalry adjutant asked.

'A dog who wants to go home,' said Kenneth.

'Sounds more like a wild banshee.'

Toby came running over to the bars of his cage and started barking as they went in.

'I'm looking for a small dog,' the cavalry adjutant said.

Toby whined as they continued on past him.

'Now this one looks like a very good candidate,' the officer said, stopping to look at a Jack Russell two cages further along from the now howling Toby. 'Let's see how he walks on his lead.'

Kenneth clipped a lead to the small dog's collar. But as soon as the dog was out of its cage it started pulling like mad on the lead and then twisted round and started biting at it.

'I need a dog who's good on a leash. One

we can take out on parade and be proud of,' the cavalry adjutant said as Kenneth returned the Jack Russell to its cage.

The next dog was so excited to be let out that he leapt up at the adjutant's face and licked his nose.

'The colonel won't like that.'

A wolfhound a little further along stood on his back legs and put his front paws on the bars on his cage. The cavalry adjutant jumped back in surprise.

'Just saying hello,' Kenneth told him mildly.

But the man wasn't listening to him. He'd stopped at the next cage.

'This one,' he said as he looked at the puppy cuddled up to his ball.

'Oh no, not that one, sir,' Kenneth said.

'Why not? Does he have a ferocious nature? Is he a bit of a biter?'

Kenneth was riled by this insult to Sammy. 'Indeed he is not. He's the exact opposite in fact.'

'Good – then I'll take him.'

'There's lots of other dogs . . .'

'I've seen the one I want and I have to get on. We're leaving for the front any day and there's no time to lose.'

Kenneth sighed and opened the cage door.

'His name's Sammy,' he said.

Sammy yawned as Kenneth clipped a lead to his collar. He trotted obediently up and down past the other dogs in their cages with the soldier.

The cavalry adjutant was very impressed with how well Sammy walked on his lead.

'He's perfect. Do you know what he's like around horses?' he asked.

Kenneth didn't.

'Never mind. I'm sure he'll be fine.'

Chapter 13

'*Was ist das?*' the young German sniper asked, looking through his periscope out at no-man's-land.

The German soldiers had heard rumours that the British soldiers did all sorts of nasty things and were very sneaky, but now it looked as if a cat was heading towards them from the British trench.

Could it be a trick? A trick to draw them out? A spy cat or worse: a cat with explosives strapped to it, or a cat with rabies . . .

You could never tell what the British might do.

Mouser saw the periscope move with her sharp eyes and went to investigate. She peered over the top of the German trench and saw the soldiers cowering away from her below. None of them seemed eager to stroke her and that just made her want to be stroked. She slipped down into the trench and headed towards the men as they backed away from her. She looked just like a perfectly ordinary grey tabby cat, but they couldn't be completely sure.

'Miaow,' said Mouser, and then she miaowed again. She was tired and she was hungry, and her coat had far more mud on it than she liked. One of the soldiers put a tin plate with some sliced sausage on the ground and then backed away quickly without even trying to touch her.

The smell of the food was too much for Mouser to resist and she hurried to the plate and started to eat.

'Looks like an ordinary cat and eats like an ordinary cat,' the soldiers told each other in German as they watched Mouser eating.

One of the soldiers took a step towards her, but the sergeant wanted to be completely sure the cat was safe to touch before his men got too close.

'Halt!' he told the soldier and the soldier immediately stopped dead.

Mouser looked up briefly before putting her head back down to finish her meal. Once the sausage was gone, she began to lick her forepaws and wash the mud and dirt away from her coat as best she could while the soldiers watched.

'Looks like an ordinary cat, eats like an ordinary cat and washes like an ordinary cat,' the soldiers told each other. They were almost positive Mouser was safe, but still they hesitated because they knew she'd come from the British trench. After she'd cleaned herself, Mouser hopped on to one of the sleeping shelves the soldiers had cut into the side of the trench, kneaded the blanket and sacking that already lay there, curled up and very soon fell fast asleep, exhausted from her ordeal.

One by one the German soldiers took it in turns to watch her and finally it was decided that the cat was safe to stroke, and when Mouser woke a few hours later everyone wanted to do so.

'Mietze, Mietze,' they called to her.

Soon they began to wonder if the cat might be good at rat-catching, as they had the same problem with rats that the British did.

'*Ratten?*' they asked her.

Mouser yawned and stretched out her claws. She didn't know what these men were saying, she didn't recognize any of the sounds, but she was glad to have found somewhere comfy to rest where she was well fed and stroked.

*

The cavalry, meanwhile, were treating Sammy very well at their HQ in Whitehall. He'd slept on a pillow with a soft blanket covering him and when he woke up he was given liver and kidneys for breakfast. He gobbled it all up just before the man in charge arrived.

'What a fine little chap he is,' the colonel said as Sammy trotted over to him and wagged his tail. 'What's his name?'

'They've been calling him Sammy, sir,' his adjutant said.

'Then so will we. Don't want him getting confused.'

The colonel stroked Sammy and Sammy licked him on his face, under his nose, where he had fur. The man laughed. 'I've already completed my morning ablutions, thank you!'

Sammy was sure laughing meant the man liked being licked very much and so he did it some more.

'We'll need to get Sammy measured up for

a proper collar and a bandana in the regiment's colours,' the colonel said to his adjutant. 'And I want my saddle adjusted so he can ride with me into battle.'

'Yes, sir,' the harried adjutant said, and he hurried out to give the orders.

'There's someone I want you to meet,' the colonel said as he picked Sammy up and tucked him under his arm. 'She's in the stables.'

Sammy looked about him as the colonel carried him into the stable building. The air was full of very interesting new smells.

Suddenly a horse neighed at him and Sammy yelped in surprise. He'd only ever seen one horse up close before, but in the stables there were lots of them putting their great heads over their doors and blowing and neighing. He cringed back when one of them, a huge chestnut mare, shook her head, sending flecks of spittle about.

'It's all right,' the colonel said as he stroked

Sammy. 'There's nothing to fear here.' He put his hand out and rubbed the white blaze down the chestnut mare's forehead. 'This is Dobby. Dobby, meet Sammy. Sammy, this is my horse Dobby. I want the two of you to be the best of friends.'

For a moment the two animals looked directly in each other's eyes and Sammy's fear disappeared. He wagged his tail as Dobby blew gently through her nose at him.

Chapter 14

Arthur and Lizzie hurried round to Sammy's kennel on Saturday morning. But Sammy wasn't there.

'Maybe someone else is taking him for a walk,' Arthur said. He couldn't keep the disappointment out of his voice. He thought of Sammy as their special charge and was looking forward to playing football with him again.

Kenneth came over to them, his face grim.

'Where's . . .' Lizzie started to ask, but her voice trailed off as Kenneth shook his head.

'Has something happened to Sammy?'

'He seemed fine when we left him, not sick at all.'

'He's gone,' Kenneth said, and he took Oliver's football out of the kennel and gave it to them.

'Gone?' Lizzie asked as she took back the ball. 'What do you mean?'

Kenneth sighed. 'I tried to get him to take another dog instead. But he wasn't having it. Sammy was the one he wanted and so Sammy's the one he got.'

'Who?' Arthur asked. 'Who's got Sammy?'

'The cavalry. He's gone to be a cavalry mascot.'

'No,' Lizzie said. 'I don't understand.'

''Fraid so. I didn't want to let him go, but the truth is he'll make a fine mascot. Pets as well as people have got to do their part.'

'But he's so little,' Lizzie said.

'They'll take good care of him,' Kenneth

said, and he was sure they would. 'The soldier that took him seemed very taken with him and I'm sure his commanding officer, the colonel, will be just as much so.'

Lizzie nodded. Anyone who met Sammy would fall in love with him. They couldn't help it.

'I'll miss him so much,' she said tearfully.

'We were hoping he could become our dog one day,' Arthur said, swallowing down the lump in his throat.

Kenneth nodded. 'There's other dogs that need your attention now,' he said, hoping to take Arthur and Lizzie's minds off Sammy. 'And cats too.'

Lizzie and Arthur followed him to meet the other dogs and cats that needed them, but they couldn't help worrying about Sammy.

'Every cat is unique, just like every dog and all animals in fact, including people,' Kenneth told Lizzie and Arthur as he opened the cattery door. 'And they all cope differently with what life throws at them.'

He stopped at the first cage. It had the name 'Jango' written on it and a black cat with a white spot on his front stared out at them from inside.

'Jango is quite a sociable cat and very talkative,' Kenneth told Arthur. 'He quite likes being handled, but will let you know when he's had enough.'

'Just like Mouser,' Arthur said. Secretly, he was still hoping Mouser might turn up at Battersea one day and they'd finally be able to take her home. He and Lizzie always looked out for her when they went out and asked their friends if they'd seen her, but so far no one had.

Kenneth handed Arthur a cat brush. 'Try grooming him if he'll let you.'

Arthur took the brush.

'Here, Jango,' he called as he crouched down

and waited for Jango to come to him as Kenneth had told them to.

'Can't force a cat so it's better to let it make the first move.'

As Lizzie and Kenneth carried on down the line of cages, Arthur scratched his fingernails back and forth on the floor of Jango's cage and the cat came over to investigate. Arthur stroked him and then tried brushing him with the soft brush. Jango really seemed to like that, but only on his back, not his tummy.

Kenneth stopped outside a tiny room that had once been a cupboard.

'Daisy and Daffodil,' he said, nodding at the room where there were two lumps under a blanket, but no other indication that there were any cats in there. The cat basket in the corner was empty.

'They've come from the same home, but have only been here a few days and are very nervous of people. Spend a bit of time with them and chat to them. If they'll let you stroke them, all well and good. But, if they won't let you, don't worry – just keep on chatting or singing to them if you prefer. It'll get them used to human company.'

'Right,' Lizzie said, and Kenneth left her to it.

Lizzie opened the door and went into the small room. 'Hello, little cats,' she said, and she sat down on the stone floor.

She thought it would be better to chat than sing to the cats as she wasn't very good at singing. At school some of the children had been selected to sing in a choir to raise money for the war effort. But the elderly choirmaster had told Lizzie she wouldn't be needed when he'd heard her voice.

One of the cats peeped out from under the blanket as Lizzie told them about what had been happening recently.

'We're still looking for our own cat, Mouser.

We're not sure where she can have got to . . .
Oh,' she exclaimed, when she saw the little face
peering out at her, 'aren't you beautiful?'

The little cat was pure white apart from its
bright blue eyes. It tucked its head back under
the blanket and the other one peeped out.

'Hello there.' Lizzie smiled, but her
enthusiasm was too much for this cat and
it disappeared back under the blanket.
Lizzie carried on talking. 'I was just telling your
friend about how our cat's gone missing. She
always used to sleep on my bed and now it feels
much too big without her stretching herself
out on the pillow.'

The cats started playing together under the
blanket and Lizzie smiled. If they were feeling
secure enough to play, that had to be a good
sign.

Kenneth came to find her ten minutes later.

'They're such pretty cats,' Lizzie said.

'They look a bit like Siamese cats to me,'

Kenneth told her. 'But they've got longer coats and haven't developed the usual markings. Want to meet your next one?'

Lizzie scrambled to her feet. 'Bye, little cats,' she said, but there was no response from under the blanket. She closed the door as she went out to join Kenneth.

'Amelia wants to take some of the pets into the hospital where she works and I think it'd be just as good for the cats and dogs we have here as it would be for the patients,' Kenneth said as they walked.

Lizzie thought it was an excellent idea. 'But not Daisy and Daffodil yet?'

'Oh no – not until they're much happier and more confident around people. Amelia has to get permission from her matron first and she's a bit of a stickler for the no pets rule. Mellie's got a meeting with her today and, although she hasn't said so, being Amelia, I know she's worried about it.'

He stopped outside a cage with a large ginger tomcat inside.

'This is Herbert,' Kenneth said. 'Now he would make a perfect hospital visiting cat. He'd be happy to just sit on someone's lap and get stroked all day long. Why don't you give him a bit of attention? You can take him out and sit in the chair there.'

He pointed to an ancient but comfy-looking armchair in the corner close to the cages.

Lizzie carried Herbert to the chair and did find him very soothing. Once he'd kneaded her lap enough for him to decide it was comfortable enough to do so, he curled up and went to sleep.

'It's most important that kittens gets lots of handling right from the start if they're going to become well socialized and make good pets,' Kenneth told Arthur as he led him to the kitten area.

Arthur spent the next ten minutes playing with some kittens that had been born at the shelter. He was glad it was a Saturday so they didn't have to rush off to school.

Meanwhile Amelia's meeting with the matron at the hospital was not going so well.

'I truly feel that bringing animals into the hospital will help the patients. Especially those who've been traumatized by the war. You know yourself how therapeutic it can be to stroke a cat or a dog.'

But the matron did not know this, nor did she agree that it was true.

'It's unhygienic to have pets in a hospital. And you're intending to bring strays in. What if one of them had the rabies infection?'

'That's hardly likely –' Amelia started to say, but the matron continued.

'And, as for a cat bite, they don't even need to have rabies to cause extreme infection.'

'Second only to being bitten by a human,' Amelia agreed. Human bites were the most dangerous. 'But these will be very calm cats and dogs and there'll be no risk of anyone getting bitten. Out on the front animals are bravely doing their bit every day, you know. There are messenger dogs and mercy dogs risking their lives to help the soldiers.'

'I've not heard of such things,' said her matron curtly.

'Britain doesn't have them yet, but the French and Belgian and German armies do and no doubt we will soon. Mercy dogs find injured soldiers on the battlefield. They provide them with medical supplies that are strapped to their bodies in a bag with a red cross on it. They even have small canteens of water tied across their chests so the soldiers can have a drink. I've read about one French Red Cross dog called Captain, who located thirty wounded men in a single day by taking one of the wounded soldier's caps back to HQ for help and then leading the rescue party right to them. And –'

'I'm sorry,' the matron interrupted Amelia, 'but I simply cannot allow animals in the hospital.' She didn't add that she herself had been bitten by her grandmother's dog as a child and had never felt comfortable around them ever since.

'But –'

'That'll be all.'

Amelia left the matron's office feeling very frustrated that her suggestions weren't being properly considered. All sorts of different treatments were being tried to help heal the traumatized and often shell-shocked soldiers and get them back to the front as soon as possible. She knew that spending time with a calm pet would do nothing but help. Why would no one listen?

Chapter 15

Sammy liked Dobby the chestnut mare very much and wasn't frightened of her at all when he had all four paws on the ground. But it was a different matter when he was perched high up on Dobby's back in the saddle pocket that had been made for him, wearing his regimental bandana. He could feel the heat coming from her body, and her chest rising and falling as she breathed in and out, and then she'd snort, and her hooves would move very fast and thump and thunder on the ground. He didn't like that. Not even a little bit.

The colonel didn't realize quite how frightened Sammy was until after they'd been riding for the first time together, because Sammy had been willing enough to sit in the saddle when Dobby was standing still. But, when he lifted Sammy down from the saddle after the ride, he found the little dog couldn't stop shaking and he whined and whimpered.

'It's not so bad,' the colonel said. 'You'll get used to it and very soon you'll like it.' But even as the colonel said the words he didn't totally believe them.

As soon as the colonel put Sammy down on the ground, he ran away back to his pillow bed and hid under it.

The next day Sammy and the colonel and the rest of the cavalry and the horses boarded a ship for the front. It was the first time Sammy had ever seen the sea. He looked down at it suspiciously from the colonel's arms.

When they docked and left the ship, Sammy tried to taste some of the big wavy water, but the colonel told him: 'No, that's not for drinking – too salty, old boy.'

Oliver spent a lot of his time digging to maintain the trenches. So much so that he often thought he wouldn't mind at all if he never saw a shovel again once the war was over. Everyone hated the mud that got everywhere, and now the rains had come it was even worse. But they dug on even when their hands were covered in blisters.

The Battersea Beasts had been moved up from the support trench line to the front-line trench a few days before.

'What's that?' Oliver asked Patrick, putting his shovel down.

'Don't let the sarge see you stop digging,' warned Patrick.

'Listen, I can hear voices from over there – out across no-man's land. I think it's the Germans.'

The afternoon sun was disappearing in the sky; there had been no action that day and it felt eerily quiet.

Oliver couldn't understand what the Germans were saying, but they didn't sound happy.

'Probably complaining about all the trench digging they have to do too,' he said as he and Patrick dug their shovels deep into the squishy mud.

A few days later Oliver was on duty in the safer area behind the reserve trench when he saw the horses arriving. He hurried over to see if they needed any help getting settled.

He wasn't used to horses, but he was fascinated by them, as he was by all animals. Horses looked so majestic to him and almost regal, yet also gentle, and their eyes . . . their eyes seemed so wise and knowing. He reached out a hand to stroke the white blaze on the forehead of the chestnut mare nearest to him.

'See you like horses, soldier,' a voice behind him said, and Oliver turned round to see a colonel with a moustache standing behind him. He was holding a small dog wearing a colourful bandana round its neck.

'I do, sir,' Oliver said.

'Ever ridden one?'

Oliver shook his head. 'Never even been this near to one before.'

The colonel put the little dog down on the ground and it came trotting over to Oliver.

'This is Dobby,' the colonel said as the chestnut mare nuzzled her face to his.

Oliver bent down to stroke the little dog.

'And that's Sammy, our mascot.'

'Hello, Sammy,' said Oliver.

Sammy wagged his tail.

'He's a bit frightened of horses to tell you

the truth,' the colonel told Oliver. 'Which is a bit of a problem for a cavalry mascot dog.'

'Well, they are a lot bigger than him!' Oliver grinned.

Just then there was a shout from Patrick.

'Hey, Ollie, look what the cavalry brought with them.'

Patrick was holding up a leather football. 'They've challenged us to a match.'

Oliver looked back at the colonel. It seemed rude to just leave, but he did want to be part of the cavalry against the Battersea Beasts football match.

'Go on then,' the colonel said, and Oliver ran over to the improvised pitch.

When Sammy saw Patrick throw the ball to Oliver, he barked and raced towards it as fast as he could. Oliver and the other soldiers watched, astonished, as he started running with the ball. Sammy was in his element, but the soldiers were worried he might bite it and ruin it.

'Get that off him!' the sergeant shouted, and the men ran after the little dog, which Sammy thought was all part of the game. A ball and people running about, calling to him and waving their arms happily – what could be better? He ran on as soldiers swerved and dived, leapt and fell in an attempt to catch him and the ball. Sammy raced in and out and behind them and even through the soldiers' legs.

'Get that ball!'

'We're trying, sir!' Oliver shouted back. But it wasn't easy. The little dog was a better footballer than most people he knew – at least when it came to dribbling the ball and evading being tackled.

Twenty-two soldiers against one dog whose legs were shorter than most of the men's feet were long was hardly a fair contest. A cavalryman dived at Sammy, and for a moment the little dog lost the ball, and Patrick kicked it through the air to Oliver.

'Here you go, Ollie!'

Sammy raced after the ball and sat down on the ground and looked up as Oliver held the ball above his head so that the little dog couldn't reach it. Sammy looked at Oliver and then back at the ball. He panted, looked at Oliver and then at the ball again. He didn't want the game to be over already.

He put his paw out to Oliver and Oliver understood only too well what he wanted.

'He didn't bite the ball,' the adjutant from the cavalry said.

'No, he didn't,' Oliver agreed, and he dropped the ball and Sammy went running off with it again.

The colonel stroked Dobby as he watched Sammy and the men. The little dog was obviously very happy with the young lad and his friends. His tail wagged constantly as he made his distinctive yipping sounds.

They'd be at the front tomorrow, leading the

charge against the Germans. The horses they had with them had no choice but to go into battle, but Sammy, well, he was their mascot, with them to boost morale and keep the men's spirits up. A job he'd done admirably ever since he'd arrived from Battersea Dogs Home. A job he was doing even now as the men chased after the ball he'd got hold of and shouted and laughed as he outmanoeuvred them. Did Sammy really need to be taken into the terror of the battle that was to come?

As the colonel watched Sammy and Oliver both running after the football as if it were made of gold, he decided that he didn't.

'Look after Sammy for me,' the colonel said, coming over to Oliver when the match was over. The cavalry had won 3–2.

'Sir?' Oliver said.

'He won't be needed in battle and I'd like you to watch him,' the colonel said with a sad smile. 'I can see how much he likes you.'

Sammy looked up at Oliver and wagged his tail.

'I think it's the football he likes more,' Oliver laughed.

The colonel shook his head. He was going to miss Sammy terribly, but it was the best thing for the little dog.

'I'll be back for him tomorrow,' he said. 'Sammy can stay with you tonight. The cavalry will be busy getting ready and I worry about him being underfoot.'

'Yes, sir,' Oliver said as the colonel nodded and walked away.

Sammy watched the colonel too, his head cocked to one side, and then he barked, just once.

The colonel looked back: 'See you tomorrow, Sammy.'

'I'll take good care of him, sir,' Oliver called out.

'I know you will.'

Chapter 16

Mouser was quite happy being fussed over in the German trench. She liked the Bavarian sausage they fed her and didn't mind the bully beef either. She certainly wasn't hungry any more when she saw the rat scuttle past her, but she caught it anyway and dropped it at the German sergeant's feet.

The soldiers were over the moon when she did so and called her '*Liebchen* – sweetie' and '*Schnuckel* – darling' as they stroked her. She didn't recognize the sounds the men were making, but she could tell they were pleased with her by the way they spoke the words. She was the perfect cat, everyone agreed.

Mouser licked her paws clean as she watched the soldiers stand on their fire step and raise their rifles up into the evening sky. She jumped slightly as they shot bullets into the air, but she was slowly getting used to the loud noises that seemed to happen around her every day. Then she watched the soldiers climb back down again and have their dinner.

Mouser fell asleep curled up next to the sergeant in his sleep hole. It was part of the side of the trench that had been dug into more deeply to form a mini cabin, and Mouser had discovered it was better than sleeping alongside the other soldiers, who were often forced to sleep sitting up as there wasn't enough space for them all to lie down.

Late into the night Mouser woke to very loud cracks and bangs going on all around her. The soldiers were running this way and that, shouting and firing their weapons. She didn't understand what was happening and cowered down out of sight.

Suddenly there was a particularly loud crack and mud sprayed into Mouser's face and eyes.

The sergeant was already up and shouting commands to his men.

Mouser shrank deeper and deeper into the sleep hole until she was as far back as she could go, but even there it didn't feel safe. She crouched low, but was ready to spring into attack mode at any moment.

She stayed where she was even when the shouting and the guns had stopped. She waited and waited, until she was sure it was safe, and then she crept forward and peered out. She couldn't make out much in the gloom, but her new friends were nowhere to be seen.

Mouser heard faint voices further along the trench and crept out to investigate, only to be confronted by a large slathering guard dog.

Mouser wasn't frightened of most dogs, but this one looked particularly vicious. It growled at her and Mouser hissed back. The next moment the dog lunged towards her and Mouser yowled and jumped up on to the top of the trench as the dog gnashed its teeth below.

'Halt!' a voice shouted in German as the dog tried to jump up at Mouser.

The dog whined and looked back at where Mouser had been a moment before.

Mouser ran on and on, across the waste that was no-man's-land, desperate to get away from the dog.

Finally, covered in mud and too exhausted to go any further, she scratched at the ground until she'd dug herself a small hole and listened to the loud bangs and cracks, and the shouts of men, and watched the bright flashes that lit up the dark sky every so often. She didn't understand this place; it was so different to her home.

The next morning she took a sip from a muddy puddle and caught a large brown rat for breakfast. It wasn't hard to do because the rats were everywhere.

She looked around her and listened carefully: everything seemed quiet again so she trotted on.

'*Here, kitty* . . .' soldiers called to her in French.

Mouser looked round; once again, the sounds the voices were making were new, but they seemed gentle and she was tired and desperately wanted to find a safe place to rest. But she couldn't see any humans.

The French soldiers had seen Mouser though, through their periscope, but they couldn't put their heads up for fear they'd be shot at. They tempted her closer by throwing pieces of cheese and meat like a breadcrumb trail of food to their trench.

Mouser was glad to find that the French soldiers did not have a guard dog and very surprised to find that they had two cats there already. A ginger tomcat called Leon immediately came over to say hello by putting his head to one side of her head and then the other. And a black cat called Beau waited for Mouser to come over to him, but was equally friendly.

Mouser nestled in between Leon and Beau and finally went to sleep.

Chapter 17

Oliver liked to run early in the morning through the dawn autumn mist down the communication trench, past the reserve trench and HQ and out along the farm track, where it was safe. He was still training to be a messenger and he wanted to be the best he could; he knew how important his job would be when the time came. Sergeant Wainwright's warning that his message might be all that saved the men from a gas attack was etched on his mind. Sometimes Patrick ran with him, but more often than not Oliver ran alone. He liked it that way.

The morning after the colonel had left Sammy with him, Oliver woke early and ready to run. He was already wearing his boots as none of the soldiers in the trenches took them off when they slept.

Sammy's button-brown eyes watched him. He'd instantly woken as soon as Oliver had stirred.

'Back soon,' Oliver whispered as he stood up.

The weather was perfect for running: bright and crisp and cold. He'd heard some action up at the front during the night, but he'd managed to get a decent night's sleep all the same.

He started to run along the dirt track, slowly at first until his muscles warmed up. But then he heard a yip and, when he looked down, he found Sammy running along beside him, looking up at him, panting, as his little tongue hung out.

'You look very pleased with yourself,' Oliver said. 'We're not off to play football again, you know, and I won't be carrying you back if you can't keep up.'

But even as he said the words he knew they weren't true. If Sammy needed to be carried, he'd carry him – for a hundred miles if necessary.

Sammy wasn't used to running as far as Oliver and Oliver's legs were a lot longer than his. But even though he was panting hard he kept up as they tore down the farm track towards HQ.

When Oliver arrived at the dilapidated farmhouse that was used as HQ, everyone made a big fuss of Sammy and the little dog was petted and chatted to and fussed over.

'Who's this then?'

'What a sweet little doggie.'

One of the soldiers ran to fetch Sammy some water and they all watched as he lapped it up.

Oliver remembered how the old soldier had told him that stopping a messenger dog from doing his job was a court-martial offence. It really didn't seem fair, and an extreme punishment for a soldier who was missing his home and no doubt the dog he had there. Petting Sammy was bringing a smile to just about everyone's face and there was no doubt Sammy liked all the attention.

Oliver was glad Sammy was a mascot rather than a messenger dog, although he did very much admire the bravery and determination of the messenger and mercy dogs he'd heard about.

Sammy looked up at Oliver and wagged his tail when he'd had enough to drink.

'Good dog,' Oliver told him.

'What's going on?' an officer asked, coming out of the kitchen with a cup of tea in one hand and a biscuit in the other. He looked at Sammy and then at Oliver. He knew Oliver from his runs. 'What's this dog doing with you, private?'

'The colonel of the cavalry left the dog in my charge, sir,' Oliver told him.

The officer nodded gravely. 'I'm afraid to say the cavalry suffered some terrible losses in the battle yesterday.'

He then noticed how the little dog's eyes were focused on his hand, the hand that was holding the biscuit.

'Do you want this?' he asked Sammy. Sammy wagged his tail and then sat down and put out a paw to show that he did.

The officer gave him the last of his biscuit and Sammy gobbled it up.

'Thank you,' Oliver said.

'Any time,' the officer said. 'Where did you run from?'

'The reserve trench,' Oliver told him.

'A good run for such a small dog. Definitely deserves a bit of biscuit as a reward. I'm more than happy to give him some of these. If I'm not about when you come next time, just ask for Lieutenant Morris.'

When they got back from running, Oliver

had a long drink of water from his tin mug and Sammy had another long drink of water from a tin bowl.

When the colonel hadn't returned for Sammy by the end of the day, Oliver went to ask when the cavalry were expected to return.

'They won't be,' he was told bluntly.

'What about the dog?' Oliver asked with concern. 'He's their mascot.'

The officer looked at Sammy and then back at Oliver. 'Looks like he's your dog now – if you want him?'

'Oh yes – I want him,' Oliver said. 'I definitely want him.'

Chapter 18

When Lizzie and Arthur arrived at Battersea one morning a few weeks before Christmas, Kenneth came over to them holding a newspaper.

'Have you seen today's paper?' he asked, and when they shook their heads he showed them a page from the one he held.

On it was an advertisement asking for people to contribute to a 'Sailors' and Soldiers' Christmas Fund'.

'It's been set up by Princess Mary,' Kenneth told them.

Princess Mary was the seventeen-year-old daughter of King George and Queen Mary.

'She wants to give everyone wearing the King's uniform and serving overseas on Christmas Day 1914 a gift from the nation.'

Princess Mary had written a letter explaining the purpose of the fund.

I want you now to help me to send a Christmas present from the whole of the nation to every sailor afloat and every soldier at the front. I am sure that we should all be happier to feel that we had helped to send our little token of love and sympathy on Christmas morning, something that would be useful and of permanent value, and the making of which may be the means of providing employment in trades adversely affected by the war. Could there be anything more likely to hearten them in their struggle than a present received straight from home on Christmas Day?

Please will you help me?

'What will they be given?' Arthur asked Kenneth. But Kenneth didn't know.

'If you've got any more spare time, we could do with help collecting money for it,' Kenneth said. 'It's worth it, isn't it, for our soldiers out at the front? There's going to be a march through the centre of Battersea on Saturday, culminating in a fête at the park.'

Both Lizzie and Arthur thought it definitely was worth it.

'Now there's a new arrival I'd like you to meet. Her name's Rosie and I think she just might be the dog we need to help raise money for the Princess Mary Christmas Fund.'

They went to the dog kennels and Kenneth brought out a small, curly-coated black dog.

'Her coat looks a bit like a poodle's,' Arthur

said; he'd learnt lots about different dog types since coming to help at the home.

'But her face looks more like a spaniel's,' Lizzie said as Rosie looked up at her with huge, meltingly beautiful brown eyes.

'Now who could resist a little thing like this?' said Kenneth. 'She'll be great with a collecting tin, don't you agree?'

Rosie wagged her tail as Lizzie and Arthur nodded.

'She's not very keen on walking far, but not to worry. I thought you might like to push her in this,' Kenneth said and he brought out an old pram that he'd put ready by the door. 'And maybe pop a bonnet on her head.' He'd managed to find one of those too and put it on Rosie.

'Do you think she minds wearing that?' Lizzie asked as they headed towards Battersea High Street. She was pushing Rosie in the pram and Arthur was holding the collecting tin on which Kenneth had written 'Princess Mary Christmas Fund'.

Lizzie didn't really like the idea of dressing a dog up if it wasn't happy about it, although lots of people did dress up their dogs, and there were many such pictures of dogs and cats on people's walls. She herself had a picture in her bedroom of three cats at a tea party, dressed in clothes with a toy tea set, and pictures like it were very popular.

'I think Rosie likes wearing the bonnet,' Arthur said. The little dog hadn't once tried to remove it, so she couldn't mind it that much.

'What a good doggie,' people commented as they dropped coin after coin into the collecting tin.

'Thank you.'

'You have her very well trained.'

'It's not due to us. She's just a very good dog,' Arthur said.

'And available for rehoming,' Lizzie added.

'Really?'

Lizzie liked Rosie very much, but she still thought about Mouser every day, wishing she'd come home. And she missed Sammy and wished he could be the one in the pram instead, although he'd probably have preferred playing football and he might not have wanted to wear a bonnet. She wondered how he was getting on in his new role of mascot and she hoped the soldiers of the cavalry were treating him well.

'Hello, you two,' Amelia said, coming down the street. 'Who've you got there?'

'This is Rosie,' Lizzie told her.

'What a poppet,' Amelia said as she stroked Rosie and Rosie licked her hand. 'Stroking her would be such good therapy for my soldiers. If only the matron would allow me to bring pets in.'

Lizzie and Arthur agreed.

Chapter 19

As Mouser woke up, snuggled in between Leon and Beau, her new friends, she heard a sound coming from further down the trench. A sound that was impossible to resist. As she crept along the side of the trench, the noise got louder. Round the next corner, protected from the elements by a shelf in the side of the trench, was a large lattice wooden box.

The noises were coming from inside the box. She'd seen these birds before, back at home in the park, but she'd never been able to catch one! Mouser stuck out a paw, trying to reach inside the box.

'*Non, chérie*,' the young French soldier told her, shooing Mouser away from the messenger pigeons in their coop.

A pigeon flew on to the top of the trench and Mouser stopped and looked at it. Then she looked over at the soldier in charge of the birds who'd shooed her away. She gave a miaow.

The soldier came over to her and crouched down as he stroked her.

'I'm sorry, little cat, but these birds are too important to be a snack for you,' he told her in French.

Mouser rubbed her head against him as she took a yearning look at the bird that strutted along the trench parapet. The French soldier picked Mouser up and carried her away from the pigeon area back to Beau and Leon.

As soon as he put her down, she ran over to them.

'Play with your friends instead, *chérie*.'

Leon and Beau introduced Mouser to the cats in other trenches, although she never met the cats that had been brought over with her from Britain. Soon Mouser became a regular at French, German, Belgian and British trenches along a small section at the front. She was made welcome wherever she went as she was such a good rat-catcher.

Late at night she slipped out of whichever trench she happened to be in to join the other trench cats in no-man's-land. Some of the cats had been donated to help the soldiers, but others were farm cats who'd run away when their owners had been forced to flee their homes.

In no-man's-land the cats played together and caught rats. Sometimes they even howled at the full moon before returning to their home trench in the morning.

In the German trenches they called Mouser *liebchen*; in the French one it was usually *chérie*; the Belgians called her *lieveling* and the British called her a variety of names like Whiskers and Queenie.

Chapter 20

From the first day that Oliver had taken him with him, Sammy became his constant running companion and they always went together. Not only did they run together, but when Oliver went to sleep Sammy did too. Oliver's mealtimes were Sammy's mealtimes and most of the time what they ate was the same.

'He must know your routes backwards by now,' Lieutenant Morris at HQ said as he gave Sammy his usual shortbread biscuit. 'I wish we had more dogs like him, especially if the threatened gas attacks happen. But no one listens to me,' he sighed. 'Stuck out here and not high enough up in the pecking order to be heard.'

Oliver looked down at Sammy. He did love running and he did love Lieutenant Morris's biscuits. If Lieutenant Morris wasn't there waiting for him with one then Sammy whined and went looking for him. And Lieutenant Morris was right about Sammy knowing the routes. Oliver was sure he could find his way back from here.

'We could train him,' he said.

'We could,' Lieutenant Morris agreed as Sammy looked from one to the other as they spoke. 'But I've only got another week here before I'm being stationed along the final stretch of our battalion's trench.'

Oliver thought that might not make too much difference. 'He does like you very much, sir, but . . .' He didn't know how to say it politely.

Lieutenant Morris looked down at the last piece of biscuit in his hand and Sammy's eyes firmly focused on it. He smiled ruefully.

'Of course, he likes my biscuits more than me and who wouldn't?'

He gave Sammy the last piece of shortbread.

'I was sent three packets of these and I've still got two packets left. When I leave, I'll make sure everyone knows that these biscuits are only to be given to Sammy as his reward for delivering messages. And tell them when they run out to order in some more.'

Oliver smiled as Sammy crunched up the biscuit and then checked the floor to see if he'd left any crumbs behind.

'Come on, Sammy,' he said, and together they ran back to the reserve trench.

As they ran, Sammy caught a familiar scent on the air. It was the smell of an old friend. He stopped running and sniffed the air, then started rushing round in circles about Oliver.

He was certain his old friend had been here, but where was she now?

'What are you doing, Sammy? Come on,' Oliver called out to him. 'It's your favourite Maconochie stew in a tin for breakfast today.'

He ran on. Sammy hesitated for a moment and then ran after him. They were back just in time for breakfast.

'That tin looks about the same size as the ones they use to put messages in for them messenger dogs,' one of the Battersea Beasts said as they were eating. The stew wasn't bad hot, but they were having to eat it cold today and no one besides Sammy was enjoying it much.

'Does it?' Oliver asked.

'Yep.'

Oliver picked up an empty tin and turned it this way and that. If he just rounded off the edges . . .

'Give it here, lad,' the grizzled old soldier who'd stopped Oliver from stroking the messenger dog said. 'I'll see what I can do with it.'

Oliver looked at the tin and then back at the man.

'Used to be a craftworker once. I can make you a message tin for your dog.'

Oliver handed over the Maconochie tin.

'I'll need more than one though,' the soldier said.

Everyone wanted to volunteer their tins, but that was too many.

'Five'll be enough.'

'Thanks,' Oliver said. 'How long will it take?'

'Depends on how many shells Fritz sends over to us and which trench we're in when he does.'

Oliver nodded gravely.

'Soon as it's good enough, your Sammy'll have it.'

Sammy wagged his tail at the mention of his name.

'He's a fine little dog,' the old soldier said as Sammy went over to him for a stroke.

Chapter 21

Lizzie and Arthur were very excited about the mayor's march for the Princess Mary Christmas Fund that was coming up, and the fête that was to follow it.

'Our school choir's going to be singing at it,' Lizzie told Amelia and Kenneth when they arrived at Battersea one frosty morning.

'The women from Mum's factory are having a football match,' said Arthur.

Amelia and Kenneth were trying to select which dogs, and possibly cats if they were carried, would be best suited to participate in the event.

'There are just so many good dogs and cats it's almost impossible to choose,' Amelia groaned. 'We'll need your help on the march,' she told Lizzie and Arthur. 'There's going to be so much to do and so many animals to look after . . .'

'As well as raising money for the Sailors' and Soldiers' Christmas Fund, we can also use this opportunity to show people how well behaved and good these animals are,' Kenneth said.

Lizzie and Arthur nodded.

'We know it's unlikely anyone would want to adopt a dog or a cat with the war on, but you never know, and just seeing them in the march will show people what lovely animals they are,' Amelia told them.

'That's a brilliant idea,' Lizzie said.

Amelia beamed. 'Deeds not words,' she told Arthur.

'Deeds not words,' he grinned back.

'What we could really do with are some clothes to dress the dogs and cats up in for the march,' Lizzie suggested.

Rosie's bonnet had been very successful when it came to collecting money. And she was sure it would be the same at the mayor's march.

'Dogs shouldn't have to wear clothes to be adorable. All they have to be is themselves,' Amelia said.

'I think Mellie is right, you know,' agreed Kenneth. 'I know Rosie didn't mind her bonnet, but I'm not sure every dog or cat will feel the same and it might encourage people to dress up their pets, who might not like it.'

Kenneth was busy bandaging Toby's paw, which the dog had started biting.

'You'll only get it infected if you keep doing that,' he told him.

Toby made a groaning sort of sound and then gave Kenneth's face a big slobbery lick.

'Yes, I know. I know you love me,' Kenneth said, wiping his face. 'But no more paw biting, do you understand?'

'Why's he been biting his paw?' Arthur asked.

'It's a symptom of stress, probably from how crowded it is in the kennels, but there's little I can do other than bandage the paw and try to soothe him.'

'Poor Toby,' exclaimed Arthur. 'Perhaps we'll find him a new owner during the march.'

'Mouser's been gone for so long now, I just hope she's being looked after somewhere,' said Lizzie, swallowing back tears at the thought of their lost cat.

Arthur squeezed Lizzie's hand. He missed Mouser and he missed Oliver too. He'd been spending lots of time helping at the Dogs Home, trying to fill the hours he'd usually spend playing football with the Battersea Beasts.

*

Mrs Jenson came along to support the mayor's march too. She pushed Rosie's pram down the street behind the Scouts in their uniforms and two school bands, one of which was made up of children from Lizzie and Arthur's school.

'Rosie is such a lovely dog,' she said to Lizzie. 'I honestly can't imagine why she ended up at the Dogs Home.'

'I know. It's not right,' Lizzie said, but since volunteering at the home she'd learnt that often there seemed no sense to what animals had to put up with. 'Come on, Bertie.' She was walking with a snowy white West Highland terrier.

Rosie, with her beautiful eyes and friendly nature, was as always a hit with the public. Mrs Jenson's collecting tin was more than half full before they'd marched halfway down the High Street. Mrs Jenson felt very proud of all the work Arthur and Lizzie were doing at the

Dogs Home. It had proved a good distraction for them both as she knew Lizzie missed Mouser, and that Arthur must miss Oliver, and playing football with the team of boys, who were all now off at war.

Kenneth was following with a one-eared retriever called Polly and he'd given Toby to Arthur to look after.

They smiled and shook their collecting tins as the spectators along the sides of the street waved and called out. Suddenly one voice rang out louder than all the rest.

'That's our dog, hey, that's our dog Rover!' a little boy and his grandfather shouted, pushing their way through the crowd towards Toby.

Toby saw them, did a double take and then almost pulled Arthur's arm off as he dragged him over to the boy and the old man. There was no doubting that the dog knew them. The little boy threw his arms round Toby's big slobbery head and there were tears in the old man's eyes.

'Thought Rover was gone for good,' he said. 'Never reckoned we'd see him again.'

Kenneth pushed his way over to them.

'He was brought in to us by the police,' he said. 'Picked up after he'd been knocked over, but fortunately he wasn't badly injured and he's quite all right now, as you can see.'

The old man looked worried. 'Is there much to pay? We can't . . .'

Kenneth could see they weren't rich. But he could also see clearly that they loved Toby and, more importantly to him, Toby loved them.

'There's no charge. I'm just pleased he's going home,' Kenneth said as the procession went in through the park gates.

The mayor stood on the bandstand and welcomed everyone. There was the smell of roasting chestnuts in the air.

'Thank you all for coming and giving your support to this worthwhile cause,' the mayor said. 'Please give generously this afternoon as you enjoy the stalls and refreshments. There's a tug of war that we'll need participants for and races at the end of the day.'

'I wonder how much we've raised for the Princess Mary Fund,' Lizzie said excitedly.

'A lot,' everyone agreed.

'The soldiers and sailors should easily all be able to have a Christmas gift with events like this going on across the country,' Kenneth said.

But no one knew yet what the nation's Christmas gift would be.

Ivor and Thumbs didn't get to see the whole march or go to the fête because they were too busy signing up to go to war. They knew today would be a busy day for men joining up: patriotic events always saw them wanting to enlist and extra recruiters had been brought in from different areas for the day.

'Today's our only chance to sign up,' Ivor told Thumbs. 'These new recruiters won't have seen us before, and won't know we're underage. I reckon we can fool 'em.'

'Can we be in the Battersea Beasts battalion like our mates?' Ivor asked as they stood at the recruiters' table in the park with a line of men waiting behind them.

'Don't see why not,' the man said, writing Ivor's request on his enlistment form.

'Me too,' Thumbs, who was even younger than Ivor, said. 'I want to be in the Battersea Beasts too.'

'And you're both definitely over eighteen?' the recruiter said, eyeing them suspiciously.

'Yes,' Ivor and Thumbs lied in chorus.

'When do we leave for the front?'

'Won't be till after Christmas now.'

'That long?' said Ivor and Thumbs.

'War'll probably be nearly over.'

They'd wanted to head out there straight away.

'Lot of men wanting to get out there just as badly as you two. You'll have to wait your turn,' the recruiter said, and then he turned to the next man who was waiting to enlist.

Ivor and Thumbs celebrated their enlistment with a meat pie from the hawker stall.

Chapter 22

'Here, lad,' the grizzled old soldier called to Oliver when he came back from his run with Sammy. He threw something through the air and Oliver caught it. 'Will that do for you?'

It was the message tin he'd made for Sammy. But it wasn't just a message tin, it was a piece of trench art and Oliver thought it was the most beautiful bit of craftsmanship he'd ever seen. It was unrecognizable as having once been a tin of Maconochie stew. It had Sammy's name and Battersea Beasts embedded on it in bits of tin and other metal debris; it was not only beautiful, it was also strong. At least three tin layers thick and with a hoop for threading the tin through Sammy's collar.

'It's beautiful,' Oliver said, and it was very hard to believe that it had been made from tins and nails, bits of shrapnel and paint.

The soldier nodded and Oliver showed it to Patrick. He was about to show it to Sammy too when he saw that Sammy had gone over to the old soldier and was sitting in his lap as the soldier stroked him.

'It's like he's saying thank you,' Oliver told Patrick.

The next day Oliver decided it was time for Sammy's first solo messenger dog run. He attached Sammy's messenger tin to his collar.

'That's it, you look very smart,' he said.

Sammy wagged his tail and gave Oliver's face a lick.

When they arrived at HQ, Oliver found out

it was Lieutenant Morris's last day before he moved further along to the next section of the British trenches.

'I think I'm going to miss Sammy's visits most of all,' Lieutenant Morris said.

He gave Sammy his biscuit as usual, but then he clipped the lead Oliver handed him to the little dog's collar.

'You wait here with me, Sammy.'

'Give me half an hour,' Oliver said. Although it wouldn't take him that long to run back, he thought it'd be best if Sammy waited a little longer before being released.

'Will do,' Lieutenant Morris said, and Oliver ran back to the reserve trench alone.

Sammy wasn't happy being left behind, but he did manage to eat some more of Lieutenant Morris's biscuits.

Half an hour later Lieutenant Morris said to Sammy: 'OK, let's see if you can find your way back alone.'

He released Sammy and the little dog set off running as fast as he could in the direction that Oliver had gone.

Mouser had left the French trench shortly after her first breakfast of tinned fish, and she was on her way to the Belgian trench for her second breakfast when she saw the little dog racing along the communication trench below her.

British, French and Belgian trenches led from one to the other, but to visit the German trenches she had to cross no-man's-land. Mouser preferred to walk along the top of the trenches to running along the bottom of them where it was muddier and there were more boots walking about.

The dog she saw wasn't large like the one that had growled and lunged at her. This was a very small dog and as it ran it wagged its tail. There was something very familiar about it and as Sammy came bounding closer towards her she knew for sure. This was her friend!

Mouser quickly slipped down from the parapet of the trench on to the duckboard below and waited for him, her tail twitching.

When Sammy saw Mouser, he skidded to a halt and then he was dancing round her with excitement and sniffing at the cat and wagging his tail.

Mouser put her nose to Sammy's in greeting and then together the two of them headed on down the trench back towards Oliver.

Oliver bit at his nails as he waited for Sammy. He'd been worried about him ever since he got back to the reserve trench. So worried in fact that Patrick had made clucking sounds and when Oliver had raised an eyebrow Patrick laughed and said, 'You're acting like an old mother hen fussing over her chick.'

'Am not,' Oliver said. But Patrick did have

a point. 'You don't think he's got lost, do you? Or gone off in the wrong direction by mistake?'

'Ollie, look!' exclaimed Patrick as he saw the little dog coming back.

Then Oliver burst out laughing. The last thing he'd expected was that Sammy would bring a friend with him when he returned.

'We'll have to send him off on his own again if he's going to bring cats back with him,' Patrick said as the pets headed towards them. 'We could do with a cat around here. I'm sick of those huge rats.'

'Here, Sammy,' Oliver called, and Sammy ran to him with Mouser right behind. Oliver was very pleased to see that Sammy's distinctive message tin was still in place.

When she saw Oliver, Mouser instantly recognized him and made a beeline for him, curling herself round his legs and purring.

'Well, hello,' said Oliver. 'Who are you?'

Mouser was covered in mud, and looked so

different to how she did back home that Oliver didn't recognize her. But he was pleased the cat seemed to like him so much. Mouser purred and carried on circling Oliver's legs while Sammy wagged his tail and looked up at him with shining brown eyes.

'New friend?' the cook said, nodding at Mouser and Sammy.

Oliver grinned. 'Sammy came back with the cat on his first solo messenger run.'

'And very welcome she is too,' the cook said. 'My supplics are always getting raided by vermin.'

'It'd be good if we can persuade her to stay. There's too many rats for Sammy to keep down and, to be honest, he's not even all that interested in trying to catch them.'

The cook went away and returned with two tin plates full of bully beef for Sammy and Mouser.

'So, has it got a name?' asked the cook.

'It reminds me of a cat some friends of mine have back at home . . . But it just can't be . . .' Oliver told the cook as they watched Mouser and Sammy tuck in.

'Yeah, it looks a bit like my gran's black cat Tibbles to me too,' said Patrick.

'The Jensons' was called Mouser, but she was grey and fatter than this cat,' Oliver said. At the sound of her name Mouser looked up at him and miaowed.

'Looks like she likes that name.'

Oliver smiled. 'Mouser it is then.' The cat did remind him of Mouser, although it was so much thinner and dirtier than her. Also this cat was letting the soldiers stroke her and was being friendlier than he remembered Mouser being. Not that the original Mouser wasn't friendly; she was, but only when she wanted to be.

As Oliver headed along the reserve trench, Sammy and Mouser followed him.

'Here we are,' Oliver said to Mouser as he picked up his kitbag. 'Home sweet home.'

As soon as he sat down, Mouser jumped up into his lap and he stroked her as she purred. She reminded him so much of home and the Jenson family.

He was sitting thinking of home when Patrick came to find him. He looked serious.

'We're needed back at the front line,' he said.

Oliver sighed. 'It's not our turn to go back yet, is it? We've only just come from there.'

'I know,' Patrick said. 'But orders is orders.'

Oliver started collecting together what he'd need. He wasn't looking forward to going back, but he didn't have a choice. He threw his kitbag over his shoulder.

'Sorry, lads,' the sergeant said, but they knew it wasn't his fault. He was only obeying orders just like they had to.

'There's not room for a football down in the trenches,' the sergeant said as Sammy ran along pushing the ball with Mouser close behind him.

'It isn't doing any harm and it's keeping him happy, sir,' Oliver said.

The sergeant made a harrumph sort of sound, but he didn't say any more and Sammy was allowed to take the ball with the men as they trekked down the communication trench towards the front line.

'How long are we going to be up here for this time?' Oliver asked.

But no one knew for sure.

'You're on first watch,' the sergeant told him, and Oliver stood on the fire step with his gun ready for any surprise enemy attacks.

He couldn't understand more than a few words of German, but he could tell when the German soldiers, who were in their own trench a hundred feet away, were joking with each other and laughing, and when their days dragged miserably by – which rainy days in the trenches did. Oliver listened out as the sun sank low in the sky, hoping he might hear voices from the other side.

Chapter 23

When Lizzie went to visit the two blanket cats, Daisy and Daffodil, after school, she told them all about Mouser being missing and Oliver having found a cat similar to her.

Both of the cats peeped out from under the blanket together to listen. They were definitely less scared of her than they had been at first. But not brave enough to come completely out from under the blanket and say hello yet.

'When they do get brave enough, you could try a cat greeting,' Kenneth told her.

'What's that?' Lizzie asked.

'Have you seen how cats who like each other often touch noses?'

'Yes.'

'They're sharing their scent.'

'Oh.'

'Obviously, if you tried to put your nose to a cat's, especially a scaredy cat's, it wouldn't be a good idea, but what you could do is try holding up your finger at cat's nose height and wait to see what happens.'

The blanket cats weren't brave enough to come to Lizzie yet so she thought she'd try Kenneth's finger suggestion with Herbert. He definitely wasn't scared of people.

But when she asked Kenneth if he'd like her to spend some time with Herbert today Kenneth shook his head.

'Not today. Herbert already has a visitor. She sat with him most of yesterday afternoon and came back first thing this morning – complete with a picnic, no less.'

As Lizzie went down the corridor, she saw an old lady sitting in the ancient armchair close to the cats' cages with Herbert on her lap. She beckoned Lizzie to her. When Lizzie hesitated, she beckoned her again, more insistently.

'Have you met Herbert?' the old lady asked her.

Lizzie nodded. 'He's a lovely cat.'

'Oh yes, he is,' the lady agreed. 'Really I think he's quite unique. He understands, you know, he really does.'

Lizzie smiled, not quite sure what Herbert had understood.

'I've told him all about losing my son at the front and he looked right at me and I think he was trying to tell me something. I think he wanted me to know that everything is going to be all right. They haven't found my son yet so they don't know for sure exactly what's happened . . . I believe he's going to be coming home to me and until he does . . . well, I have Herbert to stroke and tell him all about my son and what a special boy he is.'

'Amelia's right, isn't she?' Lizzie said when she saw Kenneth a few minutes later. 'She's right about the difference an animal can make.'

Kenneth nodded. 'Yes, I think she is. Now all she has to do is convince everyone else.' He laughed. 'Knowing my sister, she'll find a way!'

At the hospital Amelia was sure if she could just distract the soldier patients, even for a little while, from thinking about the war and remembering the terrible things they'd seen, it would be a start. She'd taken some of the men to float boats on the stream that ran beyond the field at the back of the hospital. She'd taught others how to basket weave and paint, neither of which she had any talent for herself.

'What sort of basket is that?' one of the soldiers asked her, staring at Amelia's best effort.

'I believe it's called a discarded bird's nest,' Amelia told him, and was delighted when she caught him grinning to himself.

'What they need is time,' she told Kenneth later. 'Time to come to terms with it all before they're sent back over there.'

Sometimes just spending time with the men, playing cards and gently chatting to them, seemed to make a difference.

'Time's something they don't have,' Kenneth told her.

The army needed the soldiers back out at the front as soon as possible.

'Most of them are just boys . . .' Amelia said.

All the men at the hospital needed gentle care and attention, but Amelia was particularly worried about one young soldier called Charlie. Charlie showed no hint that he was listening to any of Amelia's suggestions about which card he should play. He hadn't seemed to have heard anything anyone had said since he'd arrived in the ward and just stared into space, lost in his own world. Charlie looked so young to Amelia, apart from his eyes. His eyes were old – they'd seen too much – and when she looked into them she saw such pain. She couldn't bear to think of him having to go back to war.

'That's quite a hand you've got there, Charlie,' she said to the dazed-looking soldier. 'I don't know if I can beat you with a hand as good as that.'

She forced a smile on her face and kept her voice light as if she were engrossed in the game and didn't sigh when the cards slipped from Charlie's fingers on to the bed.

If only he'd try just a little bit. But maybe cards weren't the therapy Charlie needed. Amelia bit her bottom lip as she picked the cards up and put them back in his hand.

She was so sure having pets at the hospital would make a difference that when the doctor in charge of the ward made his rounds she decided to ask him if it might be possible, rather than trying to talk to her matron again.

'Doctor, I fear if we don't do something to help this soldier . . .'

'Yes, nurse?'

'It's just he's so very low. He doesn't seem to believe he deserves to get better. If only we could give him some hope.'

'And how do you expect us to do that? He's not the only one who's seen things no one should have to see, you know,' the doctor said sternly.

Amelia nodded. It had been made perfectly clear to her every day she came to work that the men and boys who'd been sent to war and come here were not just wounded physically. The mental scars remained far longer. No one could ever be sure if they would ever go away.

Amelia told him about her idea to bring pets into the hospital.

'I'll consider it,' he said, which Amelia sincerely hoped meant she was a step closer to what she was sure could only be a good thing for both the pets and the wounded men.

Chapter 24

'Yeeuk!' Oliver shouted in horror when he saw a partially eaten rat on his kitbag. Mouser's way of showing Oliver how pleased she was to have found him was to bring him a 'gift' and leave it on his kitbag or blanket. He'd much prefer no gifts from the cat. It had been nearly bad enough to turn him off his breakfast, but not quite.

Sammy and Mouser bounced over to see what was on offer.

'It's Maconochie stew again, I'm afraid,' Oliver told them. 'This one's made from sliced turnips, carrots and potatoes, so I'm not sure you're going to like it that much, Mouser.'

'If you're lucky, you might find a stinging nettle,' added Patrick, pulling out a suspicious-looking bit of green leaf. 'I heard the cook put them in to bulk it out.'

'It's not so bad once it's heated up,' Oliver said as Mouser and Sammy sniffed at the stew.

Mouser was much fussier when it came to food. She preferred the little bits of meat from the stew to be given to her separately rather than having to find them among the vegetables. But then she wasn't ever really hungry due to the many large and readily available rats that she caught each day.

Sammy didn't seem to mind the army food at all, even when it was cold, and quickly gobbled up what Oliver had given him, licking the tin plate clean. Oliver had to stop the other soldiers from giving Sammy extra from their rations.

'He's only a little dog and just because he'll eat it doesn't mean he should,' Oliver said. But it was hard for the Battersea Beasts not to feed Sammy when he looked up at them with his big brown eyes, and virtually impossible when he put out a paw.

'He looks hungry . . .'

'Just a little won't hurt.'

'He won't be able to run if his stomach is touching the ground and he's going to have a very important job to do if the rumours of gas attacks turn out to be real,'

Oliver had said enough, and everyone promised they wouldn't feed Sammy any more, however much the little dog tried to persuade them to do so. More gas gongs had been placed along their section of trench. The empty shell casings would be hit and make a clanging sound to warn everyone – if there was time. There hadn't been any gas attacks along their stretch of trench yet, but everyone was worried about them and they wanted Sammy to be able to do his job.

Sammy was so good at being a messenger dog, in fact, that he was much better than Oliver. A small, determined dog could easily slip down the often clogged communication trenches much faster than a man could. It was hard for Oliver to pass soldiers going the other way along the trench and still keep up a running pace. But it wasn't hard for Sammy. He raced past them, often yapping as he ran towards the men, and they always made space for him to pass through.

It was the same when the food cart was blocking the trench. This could be a problem for Oliver, but not for Sammy who simply ran underneath it, barely breaking step.

Lieutenant Morris had been as good as his word and, when he'd left to take up his new role at the final section of their trench, he'd left his shortbread biscuits behind for the little dog.

Sammy raced into HQ with his messages in his tin and always found a biscuit and someone to make a fuss of him waiting. Oliver only put the tin on him when he was to take a message, so Sammy knew what was expected of him.

'You're a good dog, you are,' Corporal Bates told Sammy as Sammy crunched up the biscuit, drank some water, sat down and panted for a few minutes while a new message was written and put in his tin. Then he ran all the way back to find Oliver.

At first, when Oliver sent Sammy off with a message wearing his special tin, Mouser didn't want to be left behind and went running with her friend. But once she knew Sammy always came back, and Oliver often spent the time that he was away playing with her, she didn't try to follow him any more, and soon started travelling off on her own adventures.

Whichever of the Battersea Beasts was on

firing-step duty watched as she ran across no-man's-land, light as a feather.

'Hello, Mouser, off exploring, are you?'

'Hope you find some tasty rats to eat.'

When he wasn't on firing-step duty, Oliver played with Mouser and Sammy. Sammy couldn't play football when they were in the trenches, even though they now had a football, because there wasn't enough room. But Oliver did roll the ball down the trench for Sammy to run after and Sammy raced after it, wagging his tail and yapping excitedly as the soldiers he ran past smiled.

As winter drew in, night-times in the trenches became very cold and the attacks on both sides increased.

Oliver and the rest of the Battersea Beasts saw men who'd been injured in the attacks being carried to the field hospital by the stretcher-bearers under cover of darkness.

All of them understood that they could be called on to fight at any moment and face the same fate. That night Oliver was glad of the warmth of Mouser and Sammy lying beside him. Christmas was fast approaching and Oliver was grateful he'd have the two animals for company, to distract him from thinking about home and having to go over the top to fight, and worrying about all the talk of gas attacks. Mouser liked to lie with her head nestled under his chin. Sammy lay squeezed in between Oliver and the earth side of the trench. Occasionally a woodlouse or an earthworm would come into view, only to be swiftly swallowed by the dog as a late-night bonus snack.

Chapter 25

Mouser liked night-time in the trenches best of all. After sleeping for most of the day, she was wide awake as the soldiers were sent down the communication trench to the rear to bring up food, ammunition and water as well as medical and maintenance equipment.

The fire step was manned continually throughout the night and day. But each shift was only two hours at night usually, because of the deadly risk to everyone if a soldier fell asleep.

It was at night-time also that the patrols into no-man's-land took place.

'Barbed wire needs repairing to the left,' Sergeant Wainwright told Oliver and Patrick.

'Right, sir.'

The two friends crept into no-man's-land with Sammy and Mouser following close behind them.

Suddenly Oliver heard the crack of a twig. Patrick heard it too and they both instantly stopped dead, although the two pets didn't.

'*Chat* . . .' a voice called out to Mouser in a hiss. '*Chérie!*'

Oliver breathed a sigh of relief. The French were friends not foe.

'Her name's Mouser,' Oliver whispered to the French soldier.

'Mooser?' the French soldier hissed back. 'Like a moose?'

But Oliver didn't have time to explain. It was too dangerous to talk out in no-man's-land even under cover of darkness. Although, if they did stumble across the enemy, it was even more dangerous to draw their weapons for fear of attracting the fire of the machine guns which would be deadly to all members of the patrol in the darkness, friend or foe.

'Like a mouse,' Oliver hissed as he and Patrick moved on.

'*Une souris*,' the confused soldier muttered as Mouser and Sammy ran over to him.

Mouser purred as she wound herself round the ankles of the soldier who had shooed her away from the messenger pigeons. Sammy wagged his tail in greeting and both pets were given the last of the cheese from the soldier's coat pocket.

When the soldier headed down the French communication trench to the stores for more wire-cutters, Mouser followed him and Sammy followed her and the lovely cheesy smell.

Sammy had often run to the dilapidated

deserted farm at end of the British communication trench when he was taking messages. But at the end of the French communication trench he smelt a quite different, much stronger and more interesting scent. He and Mouser headed off down the farm track to investigate.

It was almost dawn as they went into the farmyard and were greeted by a shriek that made them race into the nearest barn for cover.

'Cock-a-doodle-doo!'

They peered out from behind the safety of a pile of hay bales only to have the cockerel's song repeated again and again.

The next moment handfuls of corn and a cabbage were thrown into the barn. Some of the corn landed close to Sammy and he tried a bit, but wasn't keen on its crunchy texture. Mouser didn't try it. She was much more interested in the three chickens that came flapping down from their perches with a flurry and a squawk and began pecking at the corn. She was just about to say miaow when she heard a grunt and slipped back behind the hay bales instead.

Mouser and Sammy watched as an enormous black-and-pink beast with a ring through its nose came snuffling towards them.

Mouser let out an instinctive hiss, but the pig took no notice of her. It was too intent on reaching its morning cabbage to be bothered by a cat. The pig chomped on the cabbage with relish, sometimes dropping leaves and picking them up again, as Sammy watched him with his head cocked to one side.

When the pig had finished its breakfast, it headed over to Sammy, fully aware of where the visitors were. Sammy wagged his tail, unsure and a little frightened, but not as much as he'd been at first although the pig was much, much bigger than he was.

He sat down to wait for the pig to reach him,

but when the pig gave a squeal of obvious delight at meeting a new friend Sammy sneezed with excitement and stood up. The two of them nuzzled heads and were soon playing together.

Mouser was too busy stalking the chickens to say hello to the pig, but when she was confronted by the cockerel and its sharp beak she ran off in the opposite direction, only to find herself face to face with a beast that was even larger than the pig. The cow lowered its head to Mouser, looked her in the eyes and gave a loud moo.

Mouser was so surprised she jumped on to the bucket of milk beside the cow as Sammy and the pig, who were now playing chase, trotted over to her. The bucket wobbled and toppled, spilling the milk which Sammy, Mouser and the pig lapped and snuffled up.

They froze when they heard whistling. The farmer was back. The pig gave a squeal as he waddled over to him. Sammy and Mouser slipped out of the barn unseen.

They ran back to the farm track and headed along the trenches until they found Oliver.

'Where've you two been?' Oliver asked them when Mouser and Sammy arrived. He was very relieved to see them. He was used to Mouser going off on her wanderings, but Sammy had never been away for so long before and he'd been very worried about them. 'I do wonder what you two get up to out there, and what you see. I bet you've got some stories to tell . . .'

Chapter 26

Ivor and Thumbs thought going to war would be a lark. Plus, they'd be paid a lot of money. More than they could get by trying to sell rat-catching cats or dogs to the dog-fighting rings, that's for sure.

They weren't exactly sure how much they'd get, but they'd heard it was a shilling a day at least and quite likely more than that. Ivor was looking forward to being rich for once.

'Ivor?' Amelia called out. 'Ivor Dawson, is that you?'

Ivor stopped as Amelia, Lizzie and Arthur hurried up to him.

'It is you,' Amelia said. 'Well, I never thought I'd see the day. What are you doing in uniform?'

'Me and Thumbs have joined the Battersea Beasts battalion. We're going to the front to join the rest of our mates. Don't want to be given no coward's white feather, do we?' Ivor told her.

'But you're so young . . .' Amelia said. He looked barely sixteen.

'Nineteen this past birthday,' Ivor told her.

Amelia shook her head in dismay.

'I thought you weren't as old as Oliver,' Arthur said. Ivor had sometimes joined in the kickabouts out in the street. He was sure Ivor was in between his and Oliver's age. A little bit older than Lizzie.

'Nineteen and that's a fact,' Ivor replied, giving him a hard stare.

'When do you go to the front?' Amelia asked him.

'After Christmas.'

Amelia opened her purse and took out the little money she had in it.

'Don't need your money,' Ivor told her as she held it out to him.

'Go on,' she said. 'I'm sure you can find something to spend it on.'

Ivor grinned his gummy grin and took it. 'Can't look a gift horse in the mouth,' he said cheekily.

'Ivor!'

'Thanks,' he said. 'Really, thanks.'

Amelia nodded as he put the money in his pocket and went off in the opposite direction, whistling 'It's a Long Way to Tipperary'.

'He doesn't look as old as Oliver,' Lizzie said.

'That's because he isn't,' Amelia told her. 'I hope that silly boy doesn't go and get himself killed.'

They passed a large poster stuck to a wall.

'*Play the Greater Game on the Field of Honour*' was written in big letters on it. There was a drawing of German soldiers behind a trench, their rifles drawn, and then a picture of what they were thinking in a cloud above them. It said the Germans believed that British men preferred playing football to protecting their country.

Arthur was outraged.

'We don't!' he said, although he and Oliver and Lizzie did love football. But not more than their country.

'It'll be all over soon, won't it?' Lizzie said. Surely the war couldn't go on for much longer. Everyone had thought it would be over by Christmas, but it was almost Christmas now and the war wasn't over yet.

Amelia pursed her lips. 'The sooner our soldiers and their soldiers get to pack up and come home, the better,' she said as they reached the Dogs Home.

She thumped on the gate and Kenneth opened it.

'Morning to you all,' he said.

'Morning, Kenneth,' Amelia said. She was still angry about seeing Ivor heading off to the front and told her brother all about it.

'They're just boys; they don't understand what it is they're going into,' she said.

'They'll find out soon enough,' Kenneth replied gravely.

Chapter 27

Mouser and Sammy slipped down into the German trench. The place was buzzing with activity, with soldiers rushing to and fro.

'*Achtung!*' said a young soldier as he hurried past Sammy and Mouser. The soldier was struggling to carry three small green fir trees.

Sammy sniffed the air. He could smell the pine from the trees. Mouser miaowed loudly at the soldier who stopped and bent down to greet them.

'Do you like the smell? We do too,' he said in German.

It was Christmas Eve and twenty-three small trees had been delivered to this section of the German trench along with candles to decorate them.

None of the German soldiers knew exactly who the cat or dog belonged to, or even which side the pets were on, but they were always glad to see them, especially as the cat often disposed of a rat while she was there.

Mouser was very partial to rat and Sammy would eat them too, although he ate the soldiers' food with far more enjoyment.

The young soldier was sad about not being at home for Christmas. No one wanted to be here. He put his Christmas tree on the parapet of the trench and when it wasn't shot down other soldiers did the same.

He then held out a slice of German sausage and Mouser hopped up into his lap and took it from his hand.

He smiled as he stroked her fur.

'I used to have a cat just like you at home,' he told her, and his eyes took on a sad, faraway look at the memory. 'She'd sit with me in the evenings and we'd stare into the fire together. It's so long ago now. I hope my neighbour took care of her as she promised to do. I hope I'll see her again, but I don't know. I really don't know.'

Mouser rubbed her head against him and he stroked her some more.

Sammy, meanwhile, was trying Christmas stollen for the first time and finding it very fine indeed.

'Don't give him too much of that – it's too rich for dogs,' one of the soldiers said.

'A little won't do him any harm.'

Sammy and Mouser sat with the German soldiers as they linked arms and sang a song about a Christmas tree:

O Tannenbaum, O Tannenbaum,
wie treu sind deine Blätter . . .

The soldiers found the novelty of the cat and little dog who were best friends very entertaining.

'Merry Christmas!' they called after them as Sammy and Mouser leapt up the trench side and disappeared back out into no-man's-land.

'Where've you two been?' Oliver asked the pets, when they finally padded back into their own trench, tired and full of food.

The British soldiers had tried to decorate their section of trench as best they could with newspaper torn up to make paper chains.

As night fell, there was even louder singing from the German lines across the moonlit strip of no-man's-land.

'Is it a trick?' Oliver asked.

'Do you think the flickering lights on those Christmas trees are supposed to deceive us about what they're really up to?' said Patrick.

'They're singing "Silent Night" in German,'

the old soldier said. 'They're not singing it very well, but I recognize the tune.'

'Let's join in, shall we?' Oliver and several of the other Battersea Beasts said.

'Can't do any harm.'

'Can't sing it any more off key than they're doing.'

Soon both the British and the German sides were singing 'Silent Night' in their own language and then the French and Belgian sections of the trench joined in too.

'Might not be the best singing in the world, but it's certainly loud!' Oliver laughed.

Chapter 28

Lizzie woke on Christmas morning thinking of Oliver, Mouser and Sammy. She hoped Oliver would have a bearable Christmas at the front. And wherever Mouser and Sammy were she hoped they were being well looked after.

'I hope the warm socks I knitted for Oliver and his card have arrived as well as his gift from the nation,' Mrs Jenson said as she cast off the last row of the scarf she'd been making and went to pour the tea.

More than £162,000 had been raised by the

British public for the soldiers and sailors. It was much more than anyone had expected and it had been decided to spend the money on an embossed brass tobacco tin for everyone wearing the King's uniform. The surface of the lid had Princess Mary's head on it, and on the lower edge was written Christmas 1914. In the corners and around the other edges were the names of all the Allies: Belgium, Japan, Montenegro, Serbia, France and Russia.

'In the newspaper it said 426,000 men and women are being sent our Christmas present,' Arthur said.

Up and down the country there'd been marches and fêtes, sports events and collections, just like they'd done in Battersea, to raise money.

'That's so many to deliver,' Mrs Jenson said. 'Plus, the woman at the post office said they'd had a mountain of warm winter clothing, food treats and tobacco put in the collection for the soldiers when I took Oliver's cards and presents from us there.'

'Good,' said Lizzie. Everyone she knew wanted to help. At school they rarely had regular sorts of lessons any more. They had lessons about the war and spent their time digging the vegetable garden on the playing field, sewing, knitting and collecting money for the soldiers.

Their teacher, Miss Hailstock, had been very pleased when she'd heard about Lizzie and Arthur's fund-raising and collecting activities and encouraged them to do more of it.

'We must all do our part in these troubled times,' she'd said.

They'd been at the Dogs Home that afternoon with their mother as the munitions factory was closed on Christmas Day.

Daisy and Daffodil, the two blanket cats, were now no longer shy when Lizzie came to visit them and ran to the door to greet her.

They didn't even mind when her mother stroked them and they'd never even met her before.

But the best part of the afternoon was when Kenneth said: 'Look who's here,' and in came Toby with the little boy and his grandfather.

'Rover wanted to say thank you,' the little boy said, his arm round the big dog's head.

'Well, I can see he's obviously enjoying being back home and I'm enjoying not having to listen to him howling or worrying about him biting his paw any more.' Kenneth smiled as he gave Toby a sliver of ham. 'I just wish all the dogs and cats we have here could find as good a home as his.'

All of them wished that for the dogs and cats at the home.

Chapter 29

The icy white morning frost and pink-and-grey sky almost turned the barren shell-struck no-man's-land stretching before Oliver into a place of beauty. There was a hush in the air as if the day was holding its breath.

Oliver woke up and immediately felt the warmth of Sammy and Mouser curled up alongside him. He watched their breath rise like steam in the cold air, before he gently stroked them awake, muttering 'Happy Christmas' as they stirred. He tried not to think about home.

At breakfast Oliver and the other soldiers were given a souvenir brass tobacco tin from Princess Mary and Friends at home.

Inside Oliver's was a bullet pencil, a packet of boiled sweets, a photo of the Princess and a greetings card with a crown and the letter M on it. The King and Queen Mary had also sent cards for everyone:

'With our best wishes for Christmas 1914. May God protect you and bring you home safe.'

'This is for you too, Oliver,' Sergeant Wainwright, who was acting as Father Christmas, said. He gave Oliver the cards and presents from Lizzie, Arthur and Mrs Jenson.

'Thanks,' he said as the sergeant called out the name of the next soldier.

After breakfast, Oliver was on fire-step duty and as he looked through the periscope across no-man's-land he could see the lighted candles flickering on the little fir trees on the edge of the German trench. He wondered what the

German soldiers were doing today, and whether they missed home too.

'What's going on over there?' one of his fellow soldiers suddenly called out, pointing towards the German area.

Oliver watched in amazement as a German soldier holding a candlelit fir tree headed towards them across the narrow strip of no-man's-land.

'Stand down!' Sergeant Wainwright shouted as the German soldier moved closer.

The soldier didn't stop walking.

'Stand down or we'll fire!' Sergeant Wainwright shouted again.

The German soldier paused to put the tree down on the hard ground.

Oliver looked back at the German trench. It looked like the German soldiers were waving from the top of it.

'Oh, come on, Sarge, it's Christmas,' he said. 'Can't you see it's a symbol of peace? I think it's safe,' and he and the other Battersea Beasts started to wave back.

But the sergeant raised his rifle and shouted, 'Stop!' In a split second the German soldier also had his rifle pointed back towards the British front line. Oliver and the other men froze, and Oliver held his breath.

But suddenly he saw a flash of movement out of the corner of his eye – it was Sammy and Mouser! Before Oliver could stop them, Sammy had bounded over the top and was running towards the German soldier, quickly followed by Mouser.

Sammy reached the man and started jumping up around him, wagging his tail and barking excitedly at the candlelit tree while Mouser stretched up to the soldier to be stroked.

Oliver and the rest of the Battersea Beasts began to laugh, and soon they could hear laughter coming from the German trenches too.

The sergeant sighed loudly. 'Go on, then,' he said with a smile.

So Oliver slowly climbed over the parapet and went to meet the German soldiers who were now running towards them. His heart was racing. He'd never met a real-life German soldier before and he was surprised that close up they looked so much like him and his friends. If they weren't wearing their uniforms, they could have been playing football out with him on the cobbled streets of Battersea.

As they got closer, a young German soldier held his hand out to him and Oliver took it.

'*Frohe Weihnachten.*'

'Happy Christmas,' Oliver said back.

Around him he heard the words repeated over and over as soldiers from both sides greeted each other and the British khaki uniforms mingled with the German grey.

The German soldier with Oliver pointed to himself: 'Marko.'

Oliver nodded and pointed to himself: 'Oliver.'

Marko nodded.

Oliver didn't know how to speak German, and Marko knew very little English, and it was the same for most of the soldiers so, as a sign of friendship, they started to exchange gifts. A German button for a British one. A hat for a scarf, gloves for gloves, a jar of strawberry jam for a jar of sauerkraut.

Oliver didn't want to give away his bullet pencil because he was certain Arthur would like it very much and Lizzie, he was sure, would think of all sorts of things to put inside the tin. But he didn't mind swapping the sweets.

He exchanged them with Marko for a candle from one of the German trees.

'*Tannenbaum*,' Marko said as he pointed at the sweet-smelling little tree.

The football was almost as big as Sammy, but that just seemed to make him like it even more. It was too big for him to hold in his mouth, but he pushed it forward with his body as he raced after it into no-man's land, excitedly yipping.

'*Fussball!*' came a shout from the German soldiers.

'Anyone want a game?' Oliver shouted into the icy air as he and Marko ran after the little dog.

Soldiers from both sides wanted to play and, within moments, more and more soldiers came to join in – far more than the usual eleven players per team. Soon there must have been fifty or more soldiers playing against each other. And not just British and German soldiers, but French and Belgian ones too.

Their pitch was no-man's land, their goal wherever the goalie with his arms opened wide was.

Sammy was as happy as could be, racing round and round, not playing on any one team, but on both at once. The ball was his prey and his prize. He even jumped up into the air to try to get it when Oliver kicked a long shot. The soldiers from both sides manoeuvred round him and were careful not to kick the little dog as he ran between them and the ball.

Mouser watched the men's legs running about, and Sammy running through them, as she was petted by soldiers from both sides. She herself was not the least bit tempted to join in and gave the occasional miaow when the play got too close to her.

But Sammy loved it and played on and off all day, with short breaks to catch his breath before the excitement of the game forced him back into it, until he was panting with exhaustion, while Mouser watched the game from different soldiers' laps.

Finally Sammy tired and rolled on to his back and held the ball in his forepaws. Oliver watched him and shook his head.

'You are one football-loving dog,' he said and the other soldiers laughed.

As night fell, Mouser and Sammy sniffed out tasty bits of food as the soldiers from both sides told them about their own pets at home, while feeding them whatever delicacy they had to offer. By the time the Germans went back to their own trench, the pets were so full they couldn't eat a scrap more.

Sammy and Mouser fell asleep to the sound of the two sides taking it in turns to sing Christmas songs – mostly off key but very loud and in a range of languages.

Chapter 30

The soldiers in Oliver's squad never disturbed
Sammy as he ran, and the little dog never
stopped running until his message was
delivered.

'I reckon he's better than a lot of
professionally trained messenger dogs,' Patrick
said, and Oliver agreed.

'Never known him not to finish the job –
although it does help when there's a biscuit for
him at the end of it,' he said, grinning.

'Message needs taking to HQ,' Sergeant

Wainwright said. 'Nothing much – just supplies needed.'

Sammy wagged his tail as Oliver put the piece of paper in his message tin. Paper in his tin always meant running and biscuits – both good in his opinion.

Mouser watched Sammy head off and then she went to visit her friends in the Belgian trench.

Sammy ran along Oliver's stretch of trench, past soldiers, many of whom recognized him, and cheered him on along the way. He then ran down the communication trench as fast as he could, past the reserve trench until he reached HQ.

'Morning, Sammy,' Corporal Bates said as he took the message from Sammy's tin and gave him a piece of shortbread as a reward for his work.

Sammy swallowed the biscuit in one gulp.

'Did you even taste that?' Corporal Bates asked him.

Sammy wagged his tail and looked up hopefully for more.

Corporal Bates was reading the requisitions note when a loud clatter made him look up. The soldier who was manning the trench phone had dropped his handset and turned pale.

'Poison-gas attack threat,' he said.

'What? Where?' the captain asked.

The soldier turned back to the phone. 'The line's not very good. I can't tell, sir. But it's imminent.'

'Find out more,' the major ordered.

'The phone's gone dead, sir.'

'Blasted nuisance!'

'We have to get the word out to the men at the front.'

'There's going to be a mass panic,' the second lieutenant said.

'They need to be ready,' Corporal Bates replied. 'They have to be warned. There are almost a thousand men in the South London battalion in this section of the trenches. We've got to get the message out.'

Sammy watched the panicked men with his head cocked to one side. He wasn't sure what was going on, but he could sense their fear. He looked from one to the other as they spoke. He was starting to wonder why he hadn't been sent back to Oliver yet, and so gave a little yelp to get their attention.

'What about the dog, sir?' the soldier manning the phone said. 'He'd be quicker and able to get through where sometimes men can't.'

'Of course! Send him too.'

Corporal Bates hastily wrote a message and put it in Sammy's Maconochie tin.

'Go on, boy, off you go.'

Sammy raced back to Oliver with it, his tail wagging, just like it always did.

Oliver gave the corporal's note to Sergeant Wainwright without reading it.

'Sammy brought this back, Sarge.'

The sergeant glanced at it and immediately called Patrick over to join them too.

'What is it, Sarge? What's wrong?' Oliver could see the situation was serious.

'It's what we feared. Gas attack's coming. I want you to go to the right and warn them along the front line that way,' he told Patrick. 'And you go the other way, Peters, and warn the rest of the battalion. As soon as it's done, send word back via the pigeons.'

The pigeon wrangler gave Patrick and Oliver a pigeon each to take with them. They were in lightweight pigeon baskets so they could be easily carried.

'You stay here,' Oliver told Sammy as the sergeant left to prepare the rest of the Battersea Beasts for the possible attack. He looked round for Mouser, but couldn't see her and there wasn't time to look for her now.

Sammy didn't want to be left behind, and as soon as Oliver started running Sammy ran after him.

'Go back,' Oliver told him.

But there wasn't time to stop and send Sammy back, especially when the little dog would only follow him again.

Sammy and Oliver ran on through waterlogged trenches and mud, round corners where they didn't know what they would find, and all the time Sammy's tail wagged as he looked up at Oliver.

'Yes, you're a good dog,' Oliver told him. He was glad Sammy was there; he just didn't want him to be in danger.

They came to the next section of trench and Oliver gave the message to the officer in charge, took a message in return and ran on. Sammy was tired; usually they stopped long before now and had a drink of water and a biscuit. But not today.

Oliver was gasping for air too, but he didn't slow his pace and neither did Sammy.

As they neared the next trench section, Oliver heard gunshots and the blast of shells just ahead. But they needed to warn the men so they ran on, although now Sammy ran behind Oliver; his little legs were starting to get tired.

Suddenly a really loud crack sounded just to the left of them. Both Sammy and Oliver jumped to the right, trying to avoid it. Before he knew what was happening, Oliver found himself tumbling: he'd fallen off the slippery duckboards, yelling out in shock and pain. Sammy didn't understand what was happening; the noises were so loud, and Oliver was lying on the ground, when Sammy knew they should be running and racing as usual.

Oliver looked down at his leg; his foot was

twisted at a very strange angle. He started to feel dizzy with the pain. Sammy nuzzled in to Oliver's chest, and reached up and licked his face.

'Sammy, I don't think I can go any further,' he said, gasping in pain from his ankle. 'But we have to warn the soldiers further along the line. It sounds like there's even more fighting up ahead,' he added desperately.

Oliver looked down at Sammy. Sammy barked back at him. *Can he do it?* Oliver thought.

Oliver leant against the side of the trench and carefully put the message about the gas attack into Sammy's tin. He then took the pigeon in the basket and strapped it to Sammy's back. Sammy looked with interest at the basket. He didn't really like it much, but Oliver kept telling him what a good dog he was so he didn't make too much of a fuss.

'Go, Sammy, go,' Oliver said once the bird was securely attached to the dog. He didn't want to panic Sammy so he tried to keep his voice light, as if there were nothing wrong, as if it were all just some new and exciting game that they were playing.

'Go on, Sammy, that's it, go on.'

Sammy whined. He didn't want to leave Oliver.

'Go!' Oliver shouted; the pain in his leg was almost unbearable. 'Go, Sammy.'

Finally Sammy ran in the direction Oliver wanted him to.

'I only hope he gets there in time,' Oliver muttered before collapsing back against the side of the trench.

Chapter 31

Sammy had run all day long and he was exhausted. His paws were cut from the debris he'd run through, his short legs and fur were covered in mud and he wasn't used to running with the pigeon crate on him, but still he ran on.

It was twilight by the time he reached the final stretch of this section of the trench and the last soldiers of the battalion.

The soldiers in this part of the trench didn't know Sammy and had never met him before. They couldn't understand what he had on his back. As he raced along the trench towards them, it looked almost like the little dog had wings.

'He can't have though, can he?'

'Never heard of a flying dog before.'

'He's certainly fast enough to be flying.'

As Sammy got closer, they saw he had some sort of basket on his back and recognized he must be a messenger dog because he was wearing his tin. Although they could see it wasn't one of the standard-issue tins.

Sammy barked at them, waiting for them to read the message as Oliver would. But the men didn't move, they were so surprised to see the little dog. Sammy barked again, more urgently.

'Sammy? Is that you?' said a familiar voice.

Lieutenant Morris had been trying to get the communications telephone to work and hadn't noticed the little dog when he arrived.

Sammy barked again and Lieutenant Morris bent down to him.

'Sammy,' he said as Sammy wagged his tail. 'What on earth are you doing all the way out here? Where's Oliver? And what have you got on your back?'

Sammy put his paw out to Lieutenant Morris. Where was his biscuit? He always got a biscuit when he'd delivered his message.

The pigeon fluttered in its crate on Sammy's back and a soldier hurried to unbuckle the basket.

'Let's have a look,' Lieutenant Morris said as he took the message from Sammy's tin.

'Poison gas!' he said. 'Poison-gas attack threat! Alert the men to protect themselves. Everyone get a gas mask on now.'

The soldier hurried out as Sammy wagged his tail and looked up at Lieutenant Morris. After all that running and pigeon carrying, surely he deserved a biscuit.

Lieutenant Morris gave him one and Sammy crunched it up.

'HQ need to know the message has been received all along the line, sir.'

'Right.'

Lieutenant Morris quickly scribbled a message on the tiny lightweight paper, rolled it up and put it into the canister on the pigeon's leg.

'Fly away home, pigeon,' Lieutenant Morris said as they released the bird and it flew upwards out of the trench and into the sky. Sammy barked.

'No need for you to carry the pigeon any more, boy. He's going to fly back home to his coop. Once he gets back, one of the soldiers from the pigeon corps will check him for the message.'

Sammy barked again. He wanted to get back to Oliver, and while Lieutenant Morris was busy releasing the pigeon and putting on his own gas mask Sammy began running for home.

'Wait, Sammy, come back!' Lieutenant Morris called after him, but Sammy had been away from Oliver for too long and he had to get back to him.

He didn't stop even when Lieutenant Morris shouted again: 'You haven't got a gas mask!'

Sammy ran on and on, round corners and down trenches, past soldiers rushing around him as the gas gongs rang out. No one took any notice of the little dog as he flew down the line. All Sammy could think of was Oliver.

But suddenly he smelt it. It was something he'd never smelt before. But he instantly knew it was bad. Then he saw it: a cloud of yellow-green gas drifting slowly towards the trench ahead of him. He didn't understand exactly what it was, but he sensed danger and knew he had to get away from it. He jumped up on to a trench step and desperately scrambled up the steep, crumbling bank, over the sandbags and out into no-man's-land.

But soon his eyes were stinging and his throat seared and his skin burnt beneath his fur. With streaming eyes, Sammy ran on and on. Not knowing where he was going, just wanting to get away from the pain and the smell of the gas.

Chapter 32

As night fell, Mouser came back from the Belgian stretch of trench, where she'd been visiting a cat called Hansel, to find Oliver's trench in chaos. Soldiers were shouting, and the gas masks they wore made them look and sound very strange to Mouser. She backed away, uncertain, and tried to crouch down as low as possible against the side of the trench.

Soon the night was filled with loud cracks and bangs all around her. She watched as the soldiers fired over the top of the trench, bayonets glistening.

Then Sergeant Wainwright blew his whistle and the next moment they were clambering over the top of the trench into no-man's land to fight the enemy. The noise was incredible as guns roared and Verey lights and exploding rockets lit up the sky.

Mouser turned and ran into the darkness, desperate to get away to somewhere she'd feel safe. That night she scratched herself a sleep hole and slept out in no-man's-land in the rain.

In the morning she returned to look for Oliver and Sammy, but the trench was deserted.

Alone in the trench, Mouser waited for them to return. She was hungry, but she didn't eat the dead rats that lay on the ground; instinct told her not to. Clouds filled the sky and turned the day grey. As the sun went down and the long day turned into night, she left the trench to go and look for Sammy and Oliver once more.

There was a rumble of thunder and the

storm that had been threatening all day finally broke. That was when she heard a pitiful whimpering and crying sound. Instantly she knew it was her friend.

Sammy was in no-man's land, shaking and whimpering. In his terror and pain he'd run into some barbed wire. His eyes were sore, and slowly his vision got more blurred until he could see only darkness around him. He was wriggling and thrashing around, desperately trying to get free, but with every move he made the wire cut through his fur into his skin.

He lifted his head and howled up at the sky in despair as Mouser raced through the rain to reach him. Suddenly Sammy felt her beside him. He smelt her familiar smell and knew it was his friend. He started licking Mouser over and over. A desperate licking as if he couldn't quite believe she was there, but was so very glad she was.

Sammy couldn't see the wire or how it was

wrapped round him, but Mouser could. Slowly she nudged him back the same way he'd entangled himself and, with one last pull, Sammy was free and sat down in shocked surprise and exhaustion.

But Mouser nudged him up again and encouraged him on, back towards the trenches they knew. She ran so close to him that their fur touched as they steadily made their way back across no-man's land together.

Chapter 33

'Have you seen Sammy? Did he survive? Did he deliver the message? What about Mouser? Was she at the trench?' Oliver asked Patrick who stood at his bedside.

The field hospital marquee was constantly busy and almost overflowing with injured soldiers. It was where Oliver had been taken for treatment for his ankle. Lots of the other Battersea Beasts who'd been in the trench when the gas attack had happened and gone over the top to fight the Germans were there too.

'No. I don't know,' Patrick said. 'I returned from my message run to find our trench a living nightmare. They're probably fine though,' he quickly added when he saw Oliver's worried face.

Oliver knew Patrick was trying to make him feel better, but he feared the worst too. How were Sammy and Mouser supposed to survive when they didn't even have gas masks to protect them?

'No news could be good news,' he said.

'Yes.'

'Promise me you'll let me know if you hear anything – good or bad.'

'I promise.'

'How are the rest of the Battersea Beasts?'

'Most of them are here being treated for their injuries after going over the top. But it would have been far worse if they hadn't had the warning about the gas attack. At least they were safe from that,' Patrick told him.

Oliver lay back down, but he still worried. He should have heard something about Mouser and Sammy by now. They'd done so much for him and the other soldiers just by being in the trenches with them, let alone Sammy helping deliver important messages. He didn't want them to have to suffer.

Slowly Oliver drifted back to sleep, only to have scary dreams.

'Sammy . . . Sammy!' he called out in his sleep.

'Shh, hush now,' a nurse with red hair told him. 'Shh. Sleep.'

Oliver did sleep, but then his dreams turned to nightmares again and he started calling out Sammy's name.

'Who is this Sammy that the soldier keeps calling for?' the red-headed nurse asked her colleague over a late-night cup of tea.

'Probably one of the soldiers who didn't make it here,' her colleague said. 'Lots of these men came out to the war with groups of their friends. It must be hard enough when someone you don't know is killed as they fight beside you, but to lose someone you might have known since you were a child is almost unthinkable.'

'Sammy's not a soldier,' said Oliver, awake now. 'He's the Battersea Beasts' messenger dog. Trained by us and one of the bravest little dogs I've ever known.'

'How extraordinary. Where did he come from?' the red-headed nurse asked him gently.

'He was a mascot with the cavalry, but the colonel didn't want to take him into battle and so he left him with me.' Oliver smiled at the memory of his first meeting with Sammy. 'We played football against the cavalry and, as soon as Sammy saw the ball, he came bounding over, wanting to join in.'

The nurses smiled too and shook their heads.

'Good little player – even though the ball

was bigger than him! And as for his best friend, Mouser the cat, well, she's definitely the best rat-catcher in the trenches, even if she does leave me unwelcome little bits of rats every now and . . .' But Oliver couldn't go on; his eyes filled with tears thinking of his friends. 'They really should have come back by now.'

Chapter 34

Ivor and Thumbs were of the opinion that everyone thought they were much older than they actually were. But the truth was everyone knew they were just boys still and much too young to officially be soldiers.

Sergeant Stoneley had seen many soldiers come and go.

'We've come to join the Battersea Beasts,' Ivor and Thumbs told him.

'Well, most of them are in the field hospital at the moment,' Sergeant Stoneley said. 'So you can't join them just yet.'

He assigned Ivor and Thumbs to the role of stretcher-bearer. Some stretcher-bearers had a lot of medical first-aid training, but there wasn't enough time to teach Ivor and Thumbs so they had just been taught the basics before they were sent out.

'Where's our guns?' Ivor wanted to know.

'You won't be fighting so you don't need guns.'

Ivor and Thumbs were not happy about this.

'How're we supposed to protect ourselves?'

'Crazy,' Thumbs muttered.

'You can't carry rifles and stretchers at the same time,' Sergeant Stoneley told them. 'Your job is to find the injured soldiers from our side and bring them back to the field hospital.'

'What about the other side's?' Thumbs asked.

'Just leave them.'

'What if ours are dead?' Ivor said.

'It's a tough job, but you've got to be ruthless.

When there are so many injured to find and bring back, you've got to make the living ones your priority.'

Ivor and Thumbs looked grim.

'You'll get used to it,' the sergeant told them. 'You might see mercy dogs out there.'

'What are they?'

'Specially trained Red Cross dogs who're doing basically the same job as you.' He didn't add that the dogs were probably doing it better. 'They wear a red cross on the medical supplies they carry and there's French, Belgian and German ones. The German ones take back the tag from the soldiers' helmets to get help.'

Ivor and Thumbs were exhausted; they had been back and forth across the mud all day, carrying injured men to the hospital tents.

'They should've given us guns,' Ivor grumbled as they struggled to lift an unconscious soldier on to their now very muddy stretcher.

'It's not right.' Thumbs agreed with Ivor. 'How're we supposed to help win this war with a stretcher?'

The man on the stretcher they were carrying through the mud groaned in agony.

'S'all right, mate. You'll be having a nice cup of tea soon,' Ivor told him.

It was back-breaking work and not made any easier by the knee-deep mud they had to wade through.

'My arms are killing me,' Ivor said as they dropped the man off at the hospital and set off once more.

'Not again,' Ivor said as the clouds opened. It had been raining most of the day as it had every day since they'd arrived at the front. 'Doesn't it ever stop?'

The rain made their job much harder.

'Gotta be time to call it a day now,' puffed Thumbs as the sun set across the sky. 'Can't expect us to keep going on like this forever –'

'Hang on, what's that over there?' Ivor interrupted. 'Is that a dog? Do you think it's a mercy dog?'

'Maybe,' Thumbs said, squinting into the distance through the rain as the light faded. He could just make out the little dog hopping about and barking in the distance, but he couldn't see a red cross on it.

'Listen,' Ivor said. 'It doesn't sound very happy.'

They heard a high-pitched barking coming from across the plain.

'Looks like he's trying to get our attention. He's circling round the edge of that large hole.'

'That's what shell blasts do,' Thumbs said.

'What?'

'Make holes like that.'

Now the barking had turned into a desperate whining.

'Come on,' Ivor said to Thumbs. 'Summin's

wrong. I think someone's in trouble and he's trying to tell us.'

As they headed towards the shell hole, Sammy ran to them and then back to the hole, back to Ivor and Thumbs and then to the hole again, barking all the time.

'S'all right, calm down,' Ivor said to the little dog as he and Thumbs got closer. 'Poor thing is beside himself with panic.'

But Sammy couldn't calm down. His friend was in trouble, but he didn't know what to do, or how to help. His eyes still hurt and he couldn't see very well, but he could hear Mouser's desperate calls and his strong sense of smell let him know exactly where she was.

'Well, I never,' said Ivor. 'Quick, grab me ankles,' he told Thumbs as he lay down on his tummy in the mud. 'There's something stuck in the mud down there.'

Mouser had slipped into one of the shell

holes that now littered no-man's land and the surrounding areas. It hadn't looked like it would be all that deep, but it was in fact very deep, and full of water due to the almost continual rain they'd had recently. The shell hole was like a moon crater and dangerous enough for a man if he fell into it.

'Quick, it's another animal I think, and it looks like it's sinking.'

All that could be seen of Mouser now was her black nose and one paw poking out of the muddy water. She'd struggled for so long that she was beyond exhausted and couldn't fight any more.

'Hold on tight,' Ivor told Thumbs. 'I don't want to be stuck down there too.'

'I won't let you go.'

Thumbs held on tight as Ivor stretched out as far as he could over the shell hole. He could almost reach the cat, but just not quite. His fingertips were a hair's breadth away from her fur, but a hair's breadth was too far.

Mouser's nose sunk under the soupy, muddy water as Ivor yelled, 'Let go of me ankles!' and made a dive for her.

The next moment Mouser was up, coughing and sneezing, and Ivor, now covered in mud himself, had her in his arms and was grinning his gummy smile up at Thumbs. Sammy was still barking and barking, running along the edge of the shell hole.

'You look a right state,' Thumbs said as his friend emerged. 'The sergeant's going to play merry hell with us for this for sure. He sent us to find wounded men not drowning cats!'

But Ivor didn't care.

'Sometimes you've gotta do the right thing, mate.'

The little dog danced round them, yapping excitedly and jumping up to Mouser who was still in Ivor's arms.

'Looks like they're friends,' said Thumbs.

'Well, he's an 'ero,' replied Ivor, nodding at Sammy. 'Saved this chap's life. Right, we'd better head back to the field hospital with this stretcher. Not sure if they'll take a cat and a dog though!'

'The way that cat's looking at me reminds me of one of those we tried to sell to the army,' Thumbs said as Ivor cradled Mouser in his arms.

Ivor shrugged. 'Just looks like a cat,' he said. 'A very muddy, smelly cat.' He could barely remember the cats they'd caught now. It seemed so long ago.

'That dog looks familiar too,' Thumbs said.

Ivor rolled his eyes.

'Where've you two been?' the sergeant demanded to know when they returned. He gave Ivor a hard stare. The boy was covered in mud and he smelt terrible. Sometimes some recruits could be more trouble than they were worth. He would put Ivor and Thumbs in that category.

'We found these two,' Ivor said.

Now it was the turn of the sergeant to roll his eyes. He should have known these boys wouldn't listen to a word he said.

'Do a mud-covered dog and cat actually look like wounded soldiers to you?' he asked them.

'The cat was stuck in a shell hole full of water,' Thumbs told the sergeant. 'It would have died if Ivor hadn't saved it.'

The sergeant sighed and shook his head. 'You're supposed to help soldiers,' he said as slowly and clearly as he could. 'Not animals . . .'

'He is a soldier, sir,' Ivor said quickly.

'What are you talking about?'

'Look, sir. He's got a messenger dog tin.'

The sergeant wiped off some of the mud on Sammy, so he could see the tin more clearly.

'Sammy of the Battersea Beasts,' he read. 'Well, I never.' He stood up. 'Right then, you two can get cleaned up and then you can clean these two up as well. I'm guessing there might be more than a few people who've been looking for them . . .'

Chapter 35

Sammy's eyesight was still a bit misty from the gas, but there was nothing wrong with his sense of smell. And now he could smell a familiar scent above the strong aroma of hospital disinfectant. He whined and slipped inside the field hospital tent flap with Mouser right behind him.

Oliver had been given a sedative and was sleeping, but Sammy knew he was nearby. He went from one bed to the next, getting closer all the time.

'Hey, what's that dog doing in here?' said one of the patients.

'Cat too. Nurse!'

The red-headed nurse came over to see what was wrong.

Sammy's nose twitched. Oliver was so close. His tail wagged and he sneezed with excitement as finally he found what he was looking for and jumped up on to Oliver's bed.

When Oliver didn't react, he sat down in surprise, then he pushed his head under Oliver's hand for him to stroke him, and when Oliver's hand didn't move he rolled on to his tummy in case Oliver wanted to stroke him there instead, but Oliver didn't do that either. Finally Sammy stood up on his back paws and rested his front ones on Oliver's chest and then he licked and licked Oliver's face.

'Sammy,' Oliver whispered groggily. 'Sammy, is it really you?'

And Sammy licked Oliver's face again and then snuggled into him as Oliver buried his face into the dog's just-washed, lavender-smelling fur.

'How on earth did you get here?'

Mouser hopped up on to the bed and purred as Oliver stroked her too and laughed. He'd been so worried that she hadn't survived the attack on their stretch of trench.

'Where have you both been?'

'What's going on?' the soldier in the bed next to Oliver said.

'Is it Sammy and Mouser?' the other Battersea Beasts asked. They'd all been worried about them.

'Yes!' Oliver said. 'They're OK after all.'

'Who're Sammy and Mouser?' the rest of the soldiers in the makeshift ward asked.

Oliver and the other Battersea Beasts told them about Sammy and Mouser and their adventures.

'Sammy warned them all along the line about the gas attack.'

'He's a hero.'

'Mouser must have caught more rats than any other cat on the Western Front.'

'And usually she leaves a bit of them for Oliver to find . . .'

'Sammy played football at the Christmas truce . . .'

'Isn't he too little?'

'He doesn't think so!'

'He even headed the ball.'

'So that's where you two got to,' Ivor said to Sammy and Mouser, coming over to Oliver's bed.

'Went to find them some grub and the next minute they'd disappeared,' said Thumbs.

'What in the world are you two doing here?' said Patrick.

'Me and Ivor signed up,' Thumbs told him. 'We're Battersea Beasts just like you now, only we're temporarily being stretcher-bearers because of you lot getting in a scrap.'

'But you're not old enough to be in the army,' Oliver said.

'Old enough to save that cat and dog you're making such a fuss of,' Ivor told him.

'If it wasn't for Ivor, that cat would have drowned in a sinkhole and that dog wouldn't have lasted much longer,' Thumbs said.

'What are you talking about?' Patrick asked him.

And Ivor and Thumbs told them the whole story and then had to tell the rest of the Battersea Beasts too. The details of their daring deed grew with each telling.

When the doctor in charge came in to do his rounds, he was amazed at the huge difference to the whole atmosphere of the ward the pets had made. He watched as the soldiers stroked them and laughed with each other.

'They should give me and Thumbs extra

wages – danger money for going in that sinkhole,' Ivor said.

'Not still trying to make money on the side!' Patrick grinned.

'We're like heroes, we are,' Thumbs said. 'We saved that cat and dog.'

The rest of the Battersea Beasts laughed, but not unkindly. They'd been at the front much longer than Ivor and Thumbs and there hadn't been much laughter recently. It felt good.

'Thank you,' Oliver said to Ivor and Thumbs. 'Thank you for saving them.'

'I'm sorry, sir, would you rather the animals weren't here?' the red-headed nurse asked the doctor as they watched the soldiers chatting to Ivor and Thumbs about Sammy and Mouser.

The doctor shook his head. 'They're more than welcome,' he said. 'They seem to be cheering the men up, so let's leave them be.'

*

The doctor was so impressed by what he'd seen he wrote a letter about it for the *British Military Hospitals Journal*.

A short while later the matron called Amelia into her office.

'Yes, Matron?' Amelia said, trying to think what she might have done wrong now.

The matron cleared her throat before she began. 'It's come to my attention . . . that is, we wondered if you knew of any very quiet, docile sorts of pets – cats and dogs – that could be brought into the psychiatric ward as therapy for the soldiers?'

Amelia realized she was staring at the matron with her mouth open in shock and quickly closed it.

'Yes, Matron. Yes, I do know of pets like that,' she said.

'It's been suggested that pet therapy may be beneficial to our patients. Only for the mentally traumatized but otherwise healthy soldiers, not those suffering from any open wounds or infections, of course.'

Amelia could hardly contain her excitement.

'Would you like me to bring them in now?' she almost squeaked.

'Well, yes, if you don't mind,' the matron said.

'I don't mind at all,' Amelia told her. 'Not at all.'

And she ran out of the matron's office and down the corridor and out of the hospital and along the street, and was quite breathless by the time she got to the Dogs Home.

'Kenneth,' she shouted as she banged on the gate. 'Kenneth, open up. We've got work to do!'

Chapter 36

Lizzie, Arthur, a red-faced Amelia and some of the other hospital staff were playing football with some of the soldier patients on the lawn at the back of Amelia's hospital. Mrs Jenson was watching from the sideline, knitting and chatting to Kenneth, who had a little black-and-white cat curled up on his lap. Every day for a week now he, Lizzie and Arthur had been bringing cats and dogs from Battersea Dogs Home to the hospital to visit Amelia's patients.

'Here, pass the ball!' Arthur yelled to Lizzie, who was dribbling it across the lawn. But Lizzie didn't seem to be listening. In fact, she had stopped moving and now stood stock still, staring at something behind Arthur.

'Sammy!' she suddenly cried as a little dog came racing into the middle of the pitch. He ran past Arthur whose mouth had dropped open in astonishment. Sammy raced on across the lawn and easily took the football from under Lizzie's foot and started running with it.

She could hardly believe that it truly was him, but she'd know the little dog anywhere and she ran after him across the pitch.

Sammy looked over at the sound of his name and wagged his tail at Lizzie before turning back to the ball. It had lost none of the distinctive smell it had the last time he'd played with it.

'It is him!' Arthur yelled, and he ran towards the dog and ball.

But Sammy had no intention of giving the precious ball up yet and he headed off the other way, yapping his distinctive yap.

Mrs Jenson laughed so much at the little dog that tears came to her eyes and she pressed her handkerchief to them. A moment later her tears of laughter turned to tears of joy as a tall, handsome soldier in uniform headed towards her, walking with a stick. She barely noticed the cat following along behind him as she ran to him.

'Oliver!' she cried as she threw herself into his arms. 'It's you, it's really you,' she said, over and over. 'What's happened to you? Are you all right? What's happened to your leg?'

Oliver held her tight. 'I'm just fine – managed to injure my ankle in a nasty fall so they've sent me home on leave,' he said. 'We went to the house, but there was no one there. The neighbours said I might find you all here; apparently Lizzie and Arthur have been busy,' he said as they joined them.

For the first time they noticed the cat with him. 'Mouser?' exclaimed Lizzie.

Mouser miaowed as if she were agreeing that yes, that was her name.

Oliver looked from Lizzie to the cat in bewilderment.

'This is *your* Mouser? I always called her that because she reminded me of your cat, but I never thought . . .'

'She's been gone for months; we thought we'd never see her again,' said Lizzie as she scooped Mouser up into a hug. Mouser rubbed her head against the familiar, tender hand. Home at last.

'This is Amelia,' Lizzie said to Oliver as she ran up to join them.

Amelia pumped Oliver's hand up and down. 'Very pleased to meet you,' she said. 'Very pleased indeed.'

Sammy ran to join them too, the football momentarily forgotten. He circled round and round them before rolling over on to the grass and rocking back and forth, his little legs waggling in the air as they all laughed.

Amelia was very interested to hear about how Sammy and Mouser had been such a help to the soldiers over in the trenches and asked if she could take them into the hospital to meet the patients.

'They've got used to seeing the pets Lizzie and Arthur have brought in from Battersea, but I'm sure they'd love to meet two animals who were actually at the front,' she said.

As they all entered the ward, the matron came to greet them and Sammy wagged his tail.

'Who are these fine-looking fellows?' she asked, bending down to give Sammy a scratch behind one ear.

Her initial uncertainty about bringing pets into the hospital had been forgotten when she saw the difference they made, and her own fear of animals had almost disappeared since meeting the Battersea dogs and cats too.

'This is Sammy and Mouser,' Amelia said as Sammy wagged his tail at the matron. 'Heroes from the front.'

Mouser hopped on to Charlie's bed and Charlie blinked as Mouser kneaded the blankets to make herself a comfortable spot and sat down.

'She's been in the trenches too,' Amelia said softly as she lifted Charlie's hand to rest on the cat. Then she gasped as Charlie's fingers moved. He was stroking Mouser. 'That's it,' she said. 'That's it.' It was the first time she'd seen him do something independently since he'd come on to the ward.

All the soldiers wanted to meet Sammy and hear about the important message he'd delivered. Oliver told them how the little dog had run all day long to warn everyone about the imminent gas attack.

'Probably saved hundreds of lives,' one of the soldiers said, and Oliver agreed.

Chapter 37

Mouser took Sammy to explore the house that had been her only home before she'd been taken to the front. Sammy trotted happily behind her as they peered into each of the rooms, and Mouser tried each of the beds, and Sammy jumped up on each of them after her.

Fortunately Mrs Jenson was downstairs making the tea as she wouldn't have approved of pets on beds, although she knew there was no way she could make Mouser do anything other than exactly what Mouser wanted to do.

But Mouser's final choice wasn't to lie on one of the beds, but in Lizzie's wardrobe. It was dark and cosy, a bit like the sleep holes she'd got used to sharing in the trenches.

A few days later that's where Lizzie found her. Lizzie was worried about Mouser. She didn't seem to be her usual self.

'I hope she's OK,' Lizzie said. 'Mouser, come out now.'

But Mouser didn't want to leave her spot inside Lizzie's wardrobe and as soon as Lizzie lifted her out she crept back in again.

'All right, stay in there if that's where you really want to be,' Lizzie said, after she'd taken Mouser out of the wardrobe for the fifth time. She really wasn't doing any harm in there, but Lizzie had been looking forward to having her sleeping on her pillow once again.

Lizzie sighed as she wrapped her hair in curling rags and got into bed. She looked over at the wardrobe where Mouser was lurking in the darkness.

'I wish you'd come and sleep here,' she said, patting her pillow. She was worried that Mouser wasn't settling back into life at home after being away for so long.

But Mouser still didn't come out. Maybe all the trauma of the shells going off and the war had left her too scared to sleep out in the open, Lizzie thought. She couldn't think of any other explanation.

Amelia had told her and Arthur that what was needed for the soldiers who came home, unable to cope with what they'd seen in the war, was time, lots of time and patience.

'No point trying to force them to forget, unless you want to be left with a man who's not even himself any more,' she'd said.

'You just need a little time, Mouser,' Lizzie told Mouser sleepily as she closed her eyes.

Inside the cupboard Mouser made a small mewling sound.

When Lizzie woke up, it was the middle of the night and very, very dark. She could hear a strange sound, a soft lowing sort of sound, and other noises, high-pitched squeaks, coming from inside the cupboard.

Lizzie ran into Arthur's room, where Oliver was also staying.

'Quick, you've got to come quick!' she called, shaking them awake. 'I think there's something wrong with Mouser; she's making all sorts of strange noises from inside my cupboard, but I can't bear to look in case something really awful's wrong.'

Arthur and Oliver followed Lizzie back into her bedroom, both still groggy from sleep. Sammy came running in behind them, wagging his tail, eager to know what all the excitement was about.

Slowly Arthur opened the cupboard door and peered in, letting his eyes adjust to the dark. Sammy headed over to Mouser in the wardrobe, but stopped before he reached her, sat down and whined as if he wasn't sure if he should approach or not.

'Is she OK? Please let her be OK,' Lizzie said.

'Lizzie, shh, there's nothing to worry about, look!' Arthur said.

Lizzie gasped as she too peered inside the cupboard. There was Mouser and two tiny wriggling creatures curled up alongside her.

'Kittens!' Oliver smiled.

'They're so beautiful,' Lizzie said as she crouched down further to get a closer look. 'Their eyes are still closed.'

'Don't you remember what Kenneth told us?' said Arthur. 'They won't open their eyes for about seven to ten days.'

Mouser made a soft sound and Sammy went to her, his tail wagging more gently now to meet the new additions to the family.

'Well, I never,' said Mrs Jenson, coming in and pulling her dressing gown around her.

'Aren't they beautiful?' Lizzie said in awe.

'Yes, they are,' Mrs Jenson said, putting her arm round her daughter's shoulders. 'Very beautiful indeed.'

'Mouser can't go back to the front now she has kittens. They'll need her to look after them,' Lizzie said.

'Don't worry,' Oliver told her. 'She won't have to go back, although I'd like to take Sammy when we do go.'

Sammy wagged his tail. He'd happily go anywhere with Oliver.

'But I'll need my football this time,' Oliver said. 'I'm not leaving it behind again.'

'What shall we name them?' said Arthur. 'The little mites have to have names.'

'How about Ivor and Thumbs?' said Oliver with a smile. 'After the two soldiers that saved Mouser.'

Lizzie and Arthur and Mrs Jenson agreed.

And so they did.

Afterword

Researching this story was fascinating but sadly not all my research could make it into the final book.

I was very sad to lose a whole section on Lizzie playing football for the munitionettes' team at the factory where her mum works. At the time there were lots of women's teams who played against each other for charity, and the matches were incredibly popular with the public. Probably the most famous of these teams was Dick Kerr's Ladies FC, which was formed in 1917 and went on to play internationally.

I was also sorry to have to cut the information about the Brown Dog Affair and the statue that was erected in Battersea in 1906 in memory of him and the terrible things that had been done to him in the name of science. The statue was taken down in 1910 following the Brown Dog riots. A new Brown Dog statue was erected in Battersea Park in 1985.

I'd not heard of the 'Cat and Mouse Act' of 1913 until my research led me to the hunger strikes of the suffragette movement. I read with great interest the 1914 Open Christmas Letter for peace written to the women of Germany and Austria, and signed by 101 British suffragists.

The Christmas message sounds like mockery to a world at war, but those of us who wished and still wish for peace may surely offer a solemn greeting to such of you who feel as we do.

And finally anyone who reads Lieutenant-Colonel Richardson's book *British War Dogs, Their Training and Psychology* cannot fail to be moved by the work of the messenger dogs in World War I and the real-life accounts of those who saw the dogs in action:

> He was coming from the front-line trenches – a little Welsh terrier. The ground was in a terrible condition and absolutely waterlogged. The little creature was running for all he was worth, hopping, jumping, plunging, all with the most obvious concentration of purpose. I could not imagine what he was doing until the dog came near and I saw the bulging message collar. As the dog sped past I could not help but notice the terribly earnest expression on his face.

Acknowledgements

Many inspiring animals and people helped me to create this book and I am very grateful to them all.

On the writing side I've been incredibly lucky to have worked with same amazingly talented people on all of my recent children's books. Huge thanks, once again, to my wonderful, insightful, editor Anthea Townsend, copy-editors supreme Samantha Mackintosh and Jane Tait. My agent Clare Pearson who's been with me through thick and thin. PR executive Hannah Macmillan, and sales team advocate Tineke Mollemans along with the booksellers, librarians and teachers who've been so encouraging. Not forgetting the many children who've emailed to say how much they've enjoyed the books and made suggestions for other stories. Thank you – it all makes such a difference.

Books shouldn't be judged on their covers alone but Sara Chadwick-Holmes has done a stunning job, as has cartographer David Atkinson. It's been a pleasure and I hope we all get to work on the next one together as well.

On the inspiration side, special thanks must go to animal loving Aunt Myra, her cat Bertie and cairn terrier dog Pele. I never got to meet Bertie or Pele in real life, although I've seen them together on the screen. When I heard how Bertie had acted as a guide-cat for Pele when he went blind I knew their story had to be told.

There are many dogs, old and young, of all

shapes and sizes at the riverside where I take my dogs Traffy and Bella for our daily walk. I was amazed one day to see a small wire-coated terrier cross pushing a half-deflated football in front of her, tail wagging like mad as she ran along making excited yipping sounds.

That dog and football found a place in my story too.

Another dog in the book, Rosie, won her role in the story through an online charity auction. I didn't know anything about her when her family made the bid so I was delighted when she turned out to have been made for the part (although I'm very glad she has a real-life family who love her lots).

Battersea Dogs Home is featured throughout the book and I'm indebted to the excellent 'A Home of their Own' for information on the history of the home, although my book is more concerned with the caring kindness of my imaginary staff and the characterful animals they look after. Dogs and cats at rescue homes were the first to be sent to the Front, and Battersea's real-life dog Jack was awarded the Victoria Cross.

Thanks also to the many other excellent local and national rehoming centres and animal sanctuaries I visited. The care and hard work of the staff and the range of animal personalities I met were astounding.

The RSPCA has a WWI Animal War Memorial Dispensary in Kilburn, London. Its dedication is:

'Knowing nothing of the cause. Looking forward to no final victory. Filled only with love faith and loyalty they endured much and died for us. May we all remember them with gratitude and in the future commemorate their suffering and death by showing more kindness and consideration to living animals.'

I couldn't agree more.

On the emotional support side endless thanks are due to my best friend and husband whose support and enthusiasm have enabled my writing to grow and develop more than I could ever have imagined.

Thanks, as always, also must go to our own dogs, Traffy and Bella; both perfect writer's companions. Always ready to get out of bed and join me at 2 a.m. when I wake up with a new idea or plot resolution that must be written there and then. Always ready to accompany me on a long meditative walk and always ready to play at the tiniest hint that I might like a fun break.

As I sit here writing this, at 3 a.m., Traffy is lying beside me on the sofa with her head on a cushion and a cuddly soft toy beside her.

Finally, *A Soldier's Friend* is very much about rescue pets and sometimes people worry about taking on pets that need rehoming. There is very rarely any justification for this worry and most rehomed pets become a much-loved part of the family, sometimes even before they've left the rescue centre.

Nevertheless, sadly many pets are still waiting for a new forever-home. Maybe it'll be yours.

  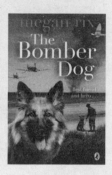

Chapter 1

London, 1940

Misty had a bed of her own, by the fire downstairs, but she always chose to lie on Jack's bed. The soft, cream-coated dog with floppy ears yawned and stretched her large pregnant tummy out across the bed and watched as her beloved owner twisted the green woollen tie round his neck and then undid it again with a loud sigh.

Twelve-year-old Amy watched her older brother too.

'Can I help?' she asked him.

But Jack shook his head. He'd have to manage it by himself once he was in the army.

'Why do things like tying ties and shoelaces have to be so tricky?' he said.

Misty gave a soft whine as if she were agreeing with him.

Amy stroked Misty's furry head and began

reciting the rhyme they'd been taught at school to help them remember how to knot their ties:

> '*The hare sees the fox and hops over the log, under the log, around the log once . . . around the log twice . . . and dives into his hole . . . safe and sound.*'

Jack grinned and finally managed to get the tie tied. But no sooner had he done so than Misty started scratching frantically at the brown candlewick bedspread, tearing at it with her paws and biting at it with her teeth.

'Misty, no!' said Jack.

Misty stopped, mid-scratch, and looked over at him, her soft brown eyes staring straight into his.

She'd been acting very oddly over the past few days – crying and hiding in corners and under the kitchen dresser, ripping Jack and Amy's father's newspaper to shreds before he'd even had a chance to read it. She'd already pulled the bedspread off Jack's bed twice and bundled it up on the floor.

Destructive behaviour like this wasn't like Misty at all. Ever since she'd been a puppy she had been a steady, gentle sort of dog.

At first, they'd thought that somehow she knew Jack was going away and this was her way of saying she wanted him to stay. But then they'd realized that Misty was in fact pregnant. Once they knew that, her behaviour seemed perfectly natural – they just had to remind her not to act like that indoors!

'She's trying to make a nest again!' said Amy. 'To find somewhere safe for her puppies to be born.'

'Good girl, Misty,' Jack said. 'You're all right.'

He sat down on the bed beside the dog his mother and father had finally got him, after years of begging, six years ago. A black-and-white photo of Misty was on the cabinet next to his bed all ready for him to pack and take with him.

This was going to be Misty's first litter of puppies and Jack was gutted that he was going to miss it.

'If only I could be here with her,' he said for the hundredth time.

But they both knew he couldn't be. Jack was eighteen and had had his call-up papers to join the army. His orders were to report to the basic training camp first thing in the morning to fulfil his military service duty. After that, he'd be going to the front. There was no way out of it.

'It's Jack who should be all jittery, not you,' Amy told Misty as Jack pulled at the green woollen tie that was half strangling him. 'He's the one going off to war. All you're going to be doing is having pups – and that'll be lovely.'

Misty pressed herself close to Jack and then crawled on to his lap as if she were still a young puppy. He could feel her heart racing. He kissed the top of Misty's furry head. He was going to miss her so badly. She'd slept on his bed every night for the past six years, ever since she'd come to live with them as a ten-week-old puppy. He didn't know how he was going to sleep without her there.

Misty stretched up her neck so Jack could scratch under her chin.

'Promise you'll take good care of her?' he said to Amy.

'I promise,' she said. 'Two walks a day and all the treats I'm allowed to give her. She can sleep in my room if she likes, but I bet she'll keep sleeping in your room as usual, waiting on your bed for you to come home.'

Jack's leaving was probably going to be hardest for Misty. She couldn't be expected to understand where he'd gone or why he had to go. All she'd know was that he'd left her.

'Make sure you give her lots of strokes,' said Jack.

Amy smiled. She knew how much Jack loved Misty and what an important task he was entrusting to her.

'At least a thousand strokes a day,' she said.

Amy couldn't imagine what the house was going to be like without Jack there. But she was sure it would be a sadder, lonelier place without him. He was six years older than her and some big brothers might not have liked their little sister tagging along with them all the time. But Jack wasn't like that. He was the best big brother in the world.

Amy swallowed down the lump in her throat. Now was not the time for crying. She had to be strong for Jack and Misty, and told herself she wasn't the only one having to say goodbye. Amy knew that hundreds of people up and down the country were saying goodbye to the people they loved as more and more men and boys were called up. They too would be frightened and worried about when they'd see each other again.

At first, the war had felt very far away from Amy's world, but no one doubted England was truly at war now. At school they were growing vegetables on the playing field and knitting scarves and socks to keep the soldiers warm. But Amy wished there was something more she could do to help with the war effort. Anything for it to be over with as soon as possible.

'I'm glad she has you,' Jack said as he stroked Misty.

He stood up and pushed his arms into the suit jacket. Then he laced up the shoes he'd polished so hard he could see his reflection in them.

'Ready to show Mum and Dad?' he said. Jack was trying on his dad's suit to wear the next morning – it felt a bit like getting ready for the first day of school.

Misty jumped awkwardly off the bed and followed Jack and Amy as they went down the stairs.

The front door was open and there was a bucket

beside it. Once a week, regular as clockwork, their mother, Mrs Dolan, cleaned the front doorstep until it shone. Most of their neighbours did the same. Mrs Dolan stood up as soon as she saw Jack.

'Oh, son,' she said, her voice breaking at the sight of her boy going off to war in his father's best suit. She clenched her floral apron tightly in her fist to stop herself from welling up. 'Your father will be so proud.'

Doorstep forgotten and cleaning materials abandoned, she led Jack to the front room where his father was waiting. This room had their best furniture and ornaments in it and was reserved for visitors and special occasions. There was a black upright piano in the corner, a floral patterned sofa, two armchairs and a print of a seascape on the wall. Mrs Dolan closed the door so Misty couldn't follow them inside as she was never allowed in the sitting room.

'Here he is, all grown up,' Mrs Dolan said as her unbidden tears turned to sobs. 'And going off to fight.'

'Hush, mother,' Mr Dolan told her, and she sniffed and wiped her tears away on her apron. 'Our boy needs you to be strong.'

Mrs Dolan nodded, not trusting herself to speak. Amy took her mother's hand and squeezed it gently.

Misty stared at the closed sitting-room door for a moment and then padded along the hallway to the open front door and sniffed. There was a lazy late Saturday afternoon feeling in the soft, warm air. She didn't attempt to go out. She'd never been tempted to stray although there'd been opportunities aplenty in the past, but the air with its myriad smells from the street was too interesting not to sniff. Next-door's dog, over-the-road's cat, the three round metal pig bins by the lamp post all made her sensitive nose twitch.

She watched as a boy emptied the scraps from his family's breakfast and Saturday lunch into one of them, waving his hand to ward off the host of bluebottles that buzzed round him.

Every few days the bins were collected and sent to local farms where they were emptied into the pigs' troughs before being returned and quickly filled up again.

Misty stepped out on to the front-garden path and sniffed. But then she heard a strange sound, little more than a hum, like a soft insect drone at first. Too quiet for a human ear to detect, but Misty heard it. It grew louder and louder. Misty hurried to the closed door of the sitting room and whined softly.

Inside the room Amy was the first to hear the distant but steady drone.

'What's that noise?' she asked.

The sound was strangely ominous and her parents looked at each other uneasily.

'What is it?' she repeated, her voice now fearful as the noise grew ever louder.

'Plane engines!' said Jack.

Outside in the hallway Misty whined and scratched at the door more frantically. Then came the sound of the siren, wailing faintly at first, but soon growing louder and louder until it was deafening. In a panic, Misty ran from the hallway, out of the house and down the front path and along the street, on and on, desperate to get away from the dreadful wailing that filled her head, thinking only of protecting her unborn pups.

As the air-raid siren joined the sound of the planes, Mr Dolan grabbed his wife's hand. They'd been warned that there could be bombs at any time, but were not expecting them just before teatime on a warm September afternoon.

'Bombs!' he shouted. 'Out to the shelter, quickly!'

The four of them ran from the sitting room through the kitchen door and out into the back garden, past the outside toilet, to the Anderson shelter at the rear. Mr Dolan pulled away the sacking he'd used to cover the small opening and helped his wife and daughter down the shortened ladder.

'In you go.'

'Misty!' Jack shouted. He turned back to fetch her, but his father grabbed his arm firmly and wouldn't let go when Jack tried to pull away.